going too far

going

too

far

JENNIFER
ECHOLS

POCKET BOOKS MTV BOOKS
NEW YORK   LONDON   TORONTO   SYDNEY

Pocket Books
A Division of Simon & Schuster, Inc.
1230 Avenue of the Americas
New York, NY 10020

First MTV Books/Pocket Books trade paperback edition March 2009

POCKET and colophon are registered trademarks of Simon & Schuster, Inc.

For information about special discounts for bulk purchases, please contact Simon & Schuster Special Sales at 1-800-456-6798 or business@simonandschuster.com

Designed by Jamie Kerner

Manufactured in the United States of America

10   9   8   7   6   5   4   3   2   1

Library of Congress Cataloging-in-Publication Data

Echols, Jennifer.
    Going too far / Jennifer Echols.—1st MTV Books/Pocket Books trade paperback ed.
    p. cm.
    Summary: Forced to spend spring break in a Birmingham, Alabama, suburb riding along with an attractive rookie police officer on the night shift, rebellious seventeen-year-old Meg finds herself falling unexpectedly in love.
    [1. Conduct of life—Fiction. 2. Police—Fiction. 3. Panic attacks—Fiction. 4. Family problems—Fiction. 5. Death—Fiction. 6. Alabama—Fiction.] I. Title.
    PZ7.E1967Goi 2009
    [Fic]—dc22   2008035158

ISBN-13: 978-1-4165-7173-5
ISBN-10:   1-4165-7173-6

For Cathy and Vicki, who egged me on.

acknowledgments

Heartfelt thanks to my editor, Jennifer Heddle, who pushed this book where I was scared to go; to Caren Johnson; and as always to my critique partners, Victoria Dahl and Catherine Chant.

going too far

1

That's the worst idea I ever heard," I told Eric. Then I took another sip of beer and swallowed. "Let's do it."

"Meg," Tiffany called after me. But I was already out the door of Eric's Beamer. My beer sloshed onto the gravel as I led the way across the dark clearing to the railroad bridge.

Eric caught up with me. His hand circled the back of my neck, stopping me at the end of the bridge. We shared a hungry look. He'd been mad when I told him Tiffany and Brian were coming along tonight. And I knew why he was angry. If we weren't alone, we couldn't do it. If we couldn't do it, what were we hanging out together for?

Now, without sharing a word, he and I understood we would do it after all. The four of us were drunk past the point of needing privacy.

In the light of the full moon I searched his handsome face a moment longer, marveled at his carefully mussed black hair. He was hot. We turned each other on. We were about to screw on a railroad bridge. It was a shame we didn't like each other very much.

I gazed to the far end of the bridge. "It's not long enough for those kids to have gotten killed on it. Seems like they could have run to one end or the other when they heard the train coming."

"You don't *believe* that story," he said.

"Party pooper. Why do you want to cross the bridge if you don't believe the story? It's not a daring deed unless you think it's dangerous."

"The girl got her shoe caught in the tracks," Brian said behind us. "That's what I always heard. And the boy got killed, too, because he went back to help her."

"That's so romantic," Tiffany cooed. She sounded like she actually meant it. She was completely wasted on her first three beers ever, way too drunk to produce sarcasm.

"And then, blammo!" I said. "Very dangerous. That's more like it." I swirled my beer in my cup. "Maybe we should take our shoes off."

Despite his party pooping, Eric took his shoes off. We all left our shoes at the base of the sign that proclaimed *No Trespassing* and offered the number of the city ordinance we were breaking. We stepped in our socks across the railroad ties, toward the center of the bridge—Eric and me, with Tiffany and Brian behind us.

Through my cotton socks, gradually I began to feel the cold, hard ties. The air seemed colder, too, as we walked farther from the riverbank.

I heard Tiffany trip, then laugh. Brian probably thought tonight was The Night, and maybe it was. He'd been bugging me for months in the back of calculus class about how to take his relationship with Tiffany to The Next Level. I had told him I wasn't that close with Tiffany anymore. I wasn't that close with anyone. He said it didn't matter. He seemed to think I was an expert on sex in general.

What did I expect? Good news traveled fast.

And I was pretty much getting what I asked for from Eric. I looked the part. As the only teenager in Shelby County, Alabama, with blue hair, I was everybody's go-to girl for bad behavior. Tonight I wore a low-cut T-shirt that said *Peer Pressure* in the hope of luring Eric into another sexcapade. As if he needed any luring. He was pretty much self-luring.

As we reached the middle of the bridge, he steered me by the neck to the metal wall of the trestle. I didn't mind being held around the back of the neck, but I minded being steered. The rich, dirty scents of rust and tar made me dizzy. I was about to shake him off when he slid his hand down to my butt and parked me against the wall.

I sipped beer and gripped the rusty wall with my other hand, looking down at the reflection of the white moon in the black river so far below us. Trees clung to the sides of the gorge, their tiny spring leaves glinting white with moonlight. People had said the view from the bridge was beautiful, but no one seemed to have actually seen it. Now I had seen it.

Now I had seen *everything*. Brian Johnson, salutatorian, math team captain, had Tiffany Hart, valedictorian, yearbook editor, sandwiched against the bridge wall in front of him. At least he'd taken the precaution of putting his beer down. He wore all the wrong clothes, a sure sign his parents didn't let him watch TV. She wore the right clothes, clean version, no skin in sight. His hands moved up her sides toward a risqué area and I almost laughed. Every few seconds, he glanced over at Eric and me as if he needed instructions.

Oblivious to Brian's groping, Tiffany shook her blonde windblown curls off her face and asked, "Why didn't those kids just jump over the side of the bridge? Is that a stupid question? I can't tell what's a stupid question." She was *so drunk*. I began to regret letting her and Brian, innocence incarnate, tag along tonight on my walk on the wild side.

"We're really high up," Brian said in the tone of the Professor from *Gilligan's Island*. "Hitting the water from this height would be like hitting concrete."

"Getting hit by a train is painful, too," I said. "But the girl got her shoe caught, and the boy wouldn't leave her. So they were stuck up here anyway."

"I'm telling you," Eric said, "that story can't be true. What kind of dumbass would let himself get hit by a train because his dumb girlfriend got her shoe caught?" Immediately after declaring that true love was something he couldn't fathom, he proceeded to kiss the back of my neck and work his way toward hickey-ville.

I tried to enjoy him, despite the irony. The cold March wind kissed my cleavage as he kissed me. A tingle of excitement spread through my body, and I tilted my head down to expose more of my neck for his mouth.

I'd grabbed him like a life preserver to float me through my last three months of high school. He wasn't much, but he was the only thing that kept me moving, besides anticipating my spring break trip to Miami one week from tonight. I would live as high as I could that week, which would tide me over until I graduated in June and moved to Birmingham for college. It was only twenty minutes up the interstate, but at least I was getting out of this tiny town. In the meantime, I was seventeen, a boy wanted to do me on a railroad bridge in the middle of nowhere, and I knew I was alive.

For the moment.

"Stop. Shhh." I pushed Eric's shoulder to detach him from my neck.

"What is it?" Brian asked over Tiffany's giggle.

"Shhh. Hush, Tiff." I leaned against the rusty wall, out over the distant black water, which stirred in the wind and distorted the reflection of the moon. My eyes strained, searching the dark for the source of the low hum. "Do y'all hear that?"

"No," Brian said.

My heart pounded in my chest. I hated being the cautious one. I couldn't help it this time. I looked one way up the tracks, but I didn't see the terrifying headlight of a train rounding the bend. I looked the other way down the tracks. Blackness. I considered setting down my beer and putting my ear to the railroad tie to listen for vibrations, like in an old Western. "Suddenly, I am full of fear."

Eric put both arms around me and massaged my boobs, too hard. "You're just stoned," he whispered so Brian and Tiffany couldn't hear. Even in their inebriated state, they would have been truly horrified at a mention of *marijuana*.

That buzz had worn off an hour ago, or so I'd thought. But Eric must be right. I was paranoid from the pot, and now I was drunk, too.

None of that explained the low hum in my ears.

The clearing at the end of the bridge exploded with the blue lights of the police.

2

"Move off the bridge, toward my voice," came the command, tinny through a megaphone.

I felt Eric tense behind me. We both looked away from the cop car to the opposite end of the bridge. Eric and I were a lot alike, unfortunately for both of us. I'm sure we were considering the same scenario. If we bolted away from the cops, we wouldn't have a car. We'd follow the railroad tracks to the next town, or hike miles through the forest to the next bridge over the river. We'd have to come back home anyway, and the police would catch us eventually. Brian and Tiffany would rat us out to save their GPAs. Worst of all, my dad would tell me I'd made it even harder on my mom by letting her think I'd been kidnapped, not just arrested.

Besides, I needed to stay with Tiffany. I hadn't exactly gotten her into this mess. She'd come to me, requesting a mess. But she wouldn't be in the mess now if it weren't for me. And Brian definitely wasn't staying with her. He was already following the cop's order, stepping from railroad tie to railroad tie, leaving Tiffany frozen against the cold metal wall. He probably hoped to get time off for good behavior. I never would have expected Eric to be strong for me, but for Tiffany's sake, I'd expected more out of Brian.

I took the beer cup from Tiffany's shaking hand and set down her cup and mine. The cop must have suspected we'd been drinking, but it seemed stupid to carry the beer off the bridge and present it to him. I put my arm around her. "Come on."

"Oh my God oh my God oh my God oh my God." As we walked behind Eric, she fished her cell phone out of her pocket and pressed a button.

"Who are you calling? Your lawyer?" I thought a little humor might cheer her up.

Apparently this was not the time. "Oh my God!" she screamed at me. "Mom?" she squealed into the phone. "I'm okay, everyone's okay, but I'm in trouble. You have to come to the police station and get me."

"Tiffany, turn the phone off," said the tinny megaphone voice.

She pressed another button to hang up the phone, like someone used to following orders. "Oh my God," she shrieked at me, "he knows who I am!"

This *was* kind of weird, but not impossible. It was a small town. We probably went to school with the cop's daughter. "He would have found out who you were when he looked at your driver's license, anyway," I said. "What does it matter?"

"He's going to tell my parents!"

It almost made sense. I was about to point out to her that she'd *just called* her parents herself, when Brian reached the end of the bridge.

The muscular cop with a military haircut stepped out of the shadows, into the moonlight and swirling blue light from his car. The sneaky shit must have driven all the way down here from the main road with his headlights off.

He said something quietly. Brian cowered before authority. He bent his head, gave the cop one wrist to handcuff to the railing at the end of the bridge, and spread his legs. Then he let the cop pat his hands over him, searching him. Hell, he would have submitted to a strip search if the cop had snapped his fingers.

Now Eric reached the end of the bridge. The cop didn't look quite so enormous next to Eric, who was six foot three. But Eric was skinny, and the cop was built like Matt Damon.

Eric let the cop handcuff him to the railing and search him, too. Unlike Brian, Eric gave the cop shit the whole time, almost like they knew each other. Which was likely, considering what Eric had been up to lately. Anyway, everybody in town knew Eric because his daddy was a hotshot lawyer.

I helped Tiffany sit down on a railroad tie at the end of the bridge so we could put our shoes on. The cop had his back turned, and I couldn't hear what he was saying. But I could hear Eric lying. "I'm not high. You think anybody in town would sell to me? Lord knows I've tried." Then, "It was my girlfriend's idea to come up here in the first place."

"Thanks, asshole," I called, giving him the thumbs-up. "Chivalry isn't dead."

"It was *your* idea," Tiffany reminded Eric. She squinted at me. "Wasn't it?"

"Don't say anything else to each other." The cop still spoke as he had through the megaphone, calm and cool with a threat underneath. He curled one finger at Tiffany. "Your turn."

"Oh my God." She stood and walked toward the cop. I watched her, ready to catch her if she collapsed. At least, I would try. I wasn't too sure about my own balance.

I also watched to make sure the cop wasn't a perv, but he didn't pat her down and handcuff her to the railing. He handcuffed both her wrists behind her back while she mouthed, "Oh my God oh my God." Then he guided her by the elbow into the backseat of the cop car, strapped the seat belt around her, and closed the door.

He motioned to me. My turn.

The low hum started again. Or maybe it had never stopped.

Eric and Brian both made a noise. "She has a little problem with being restrained," Eric told the cop. "I've tried that, too."

"Sounds like a good reason not to drink underage and trespass on city property." The cop walked over to me.

"She does have a real problem," Brian said. "Sir. I haven't tried it, but there was this incident in the ninth grade."

I wondered whether Brian meant the time I couldn't get my ankle untied from Julie Meadows's ankle after the three-legged race in PE, or the time Todd Pemberton trapped me between floors in the handicapped elevator.

"Stand up," the cop told me.

"Look," Eric called, "when she resists arrest, I don't want to get in more trouble for that. Remember I told you."

The cop did not care. I stood slowly, shaking worse than Tiffany. Something bad was about to happen. He was going to handcuff me. Or I was going to break down and plead with him not to.

"Turn around," he said.

Heart pounding, I faced the cop car.

Behind me, the cop grabbed my wrist. "You need to find out what this feels like," he said, warm breath on the back of my neck.

"I already know what it feels like," I whispered.

"I don't think you do." Handcuffs opened with a ping of metal.

"Oh, look," I cried as more blue lights emerged from the woods. A second cop car pulled into the clearing. Maybe the arrival of backup would distract Dudley Do-Right from his mission. "Are we that much of a threat to society? Or is it just a slow crime day?" Now an enormous fire engine eased into the clearing. Low-hanging tree branches screeched against its red lights. "Slow fire day," I added. Last came an ambulance. "Slow stroke day. Why'd you call the cavalry?"

"Thought we'd need them when you got hit by a train," the cop said.

"What train?"

The low hum escalated into a roar as the train's headlight emerged from the dark trees at the far side of the bridge. In a few seconds, the locomotive had reached the middle. Two beer cups blew over the metal wall and floated downward, disappearing into the darkness.

A few more seconds and the locomotive passed us. The engineer chose this moment to lay on the head-splitting horn. Eric and Brian, chained close to the tracks, each put one free hand up to one ear.

I stumbled a few paces before I realized the cop was dragging me backward by the elbow toward his car, cussing.

We passed a knot of emergency response personnel chatting together, disappointed there was nothing for them to do. "There's McPherson," called Quincy, the paramedic I happened to know. "I could see even when you were thirteen years old that you were nothing but trouble."

"Of all the freaking nerve!" I screamed back at him, but the cop shoved me into the car and closed the door.

I tried the handle. Locked.

Do not panic. I made myself breathe slowly. At least the cop had forgotten about handcuffing me. And I couldn't panic in front of Tiffany. Stretching the shoulder belt to the limit, she lay sideways and sobbed into the vinyl seat.

I pulled her head into my lap and wiped her wet hair out of her eyes. "Have you put the yearbook to bed yet? You could add something to the list of accomplishments under my senior picture. 'Managed to get the valedictorian arrested.' "

She sniffed. "It's not funny, Meg. They might take valedictorian away from me. They might take away our scholarships to UAB."

I seriously doubted the University of Alabama at Birmingham was watching the police blotter for incoming freshmen. "They can't even keep my name straight," I told her. "I've been getting registration forms addressed to Mr. Mac McRearson. I almost wish I was going to live in the dorm so they'd give me a boy for a roommate." But I planned to work my way through college to pay for an apartment. I didn't want to live in a dorm with visitation hours and curfews and monitors. I'd had enough of the Big Brother treatment from my parents at home. And my arrest wouldn't help that situation for the next few months.

Tiffany laughed a little, sniffed again. "I'm going to need a new boy, too, after this."

That was the truth. Now that Tiffany and Brian had been arrested together, a date at the putt-putt golf course wouldn't hold the same romance. While tank cars and flatbed cars and boxcars decorated with graffiti continued to rumble by, the cop got down in Brian's face and shouted at him. Then he got up in Eric's face and shouted at *him*. Through the rolled-up windows of the police car and over the roar of the train, I couldn't hear what he was saying. But judging from the look on Brian's and even Eric's face, it was pretty intense. One of the spectator firemen took a step in their direction as if to coax the cop to back off.

A second cop put a hand on the fireman's shoulder and held him in place. The second cop was older than our cop. Not nearing retirement age, but way too old to be wearing a patrolman's uniform without getting a promotion to detective.

The endless train behind them made me dizzy. I looked down at Tiffany, who had resumed mouthing, "Oh my God."

"We're getting off easy, Tiff. Too easy, come to think of it. Why are the boys the ones who get yelled at, like they're the only ones who matter? We should be offended."

"Then go tell the police officer how offended you are," Tiffany snapped. "Let him handcuff *you* to the bridge."

I tried the handle once more, jokingly. "Door's locked." But I began to shake again in the warm car.

"I shouldn't have said that." Tiffany sat up awkwardly and leaned her head on my shoulder. "You have a thing about being locked up. I'm glad I'm handcuffed and not you."

Me too, I didn't say. I had thought of Tiffany as a walking, talking version of Microsoft Excel, but she had more soul than I'd given her credit for.

We both jumped, probably delayed a few seconds by our hampered reflexes, as our cop opened his door. The racket of the train followed him inside. The last of the train cars had cleared the bridge. I watched its flashing taillights disappear around a bend in the tracks.

The cop shoved his muscular frame into the driver's seat and slammed the door shut. Then he said a few words into his CB, reached for a clipboard, and began filling out forms. He never glanced at us through the metal grid that separated him from us dangerous criminals. A bead of sweat trickled down the back of his thick cop-neck.

I looked for Eric and Brian and saw them in the backseat of the old cop's car, which was parked on the far side of Eric's Beamer. The dejected fire truck and ambulance eased out of the clearing and up the road without flashing their lights.

"What are you so mad about?" I asked the cop. "Is it true that a couple of teenagers got killed here a long time ago?"

"It's true," he said without looking up. "And y'all came close to adding four more to the body count tonight."

"Not four," I said. "If I'd gotten caught on the tracks, I would have been the only one killed. My boyfriend wouldn't cross the street to save my life."

"Some boyfriend." The cop drew broad strokes through parts of the form that did not apply to us, perhaps *previous convictions* or *gainful employment* or *significant other*.

"How'd you find us down here?" I asked.

"You were out of luck. Beware the Ides of March."

A wave of that paranoia I'd felt on the bridge washed over me. It *was* March 15. Then my drowning brain struggled to the surface.

But before I could make a smart-ass remark, Tiffany lifted her head from my shoulder. Her own drunken brain must have recognized the Ides of March line from Shakespeare. "Oooh, were you an English major in college? *I'm* going to be an English major!"

"At this rate," the cop said, "you're not majoring in *anything*."

It was all I could do to stop myself from screaming at the cop. Surely he could see how freaked out Tiffany was already. If she thought her college English degree was threatened, she was liable to melt into a pool of tears and beer right here on his torn vinyl police car seat. And it would serve him right to have to clean it up.

"Everybody reads *Julius Caesar* in high school," I told her, loudly enough for the cop to hear. "You don't need a college education to be a cop. What for? You just need to be able to drive. Read. Write." I watched him X through another section of the form. "Or not."

"Don't," she warned faintly.

I put my arm around her again and asked the cop, "Can you take her cuffs off? I'll vouch for her."

His eyes finally flicked up to mine. Probably because everything was a bit blurry to me, I hadn't registered his face at all before. I don't know if it was the alcohol or the adrenaline draining away, but I noticed his eyes for the first time now, framed perfectly in the rectangle of the rearview mirror. They were a strangely dark brown in his light face. He looked down at his form.

"Why not?" I asked. "Do you feel threatened? Big strong guy like you?"

He actually turned around in his seat and glared at me through the metal grid between us. One of the taunts I'd flung at him had hit home. He *did* feel threatened. What in the world for?

"Yow!" I yelped as Tiffany reached behind me with her cuffed hands and pinched a big hunk of my butt.

The cop was out of the car. He opened Tiffany's door. She scooted backward toward him across the seat, and he knelt to unlock the cuffs.

"Those boys just want to get in your pants," he said. "You know that, right?" I guessed he was talking to Tiffany. He wasn't looking over her shoulder at me.

Then his eyes met mine, and returned to Tiffany's cuffs.

"That's not true," Tiffany said.

Well, of course it was true. But if Tiffany didn't know this, now was not the time to clue her in.

"How do you know *we* weren't trying to get in *their* pants?" I asked.

The cop stopped fiddling with his key in the cuffs, sat back on his haunches, and stared at me.

Tiffany's chant of "Oh my God oh my God" morphed into "Shut up shut up."

The cop said, "You've got such a mouth that you'd get yourself and your friend in worse trouble just to have the last word."

"Some people just don't know when to shut up," I said.

"Shut up!" Tiffany wailed.

I began to think this was good advice. The cop gave Tiffany's cuffs just a few more seconds of attention. She pulled her arms free with a sob and rubbed her wrists. Then he slammed her door, rounded the back of the car, and opened my door. "Get out."

I climbed out and stood against the car, trying not to flinch when he slammed the door again. He stood directly in front of me and looked way down at me. I was about to get it like Eric and Brian.

Maybe not. His glance traveled briefly down to my *Peer Pressure* T-shirt. Or the absence of said T-shirt over my cleave. Theoretically this could have worked to my advantage. But I was unwilling or unable to Work It under the intensity of those deep brown eyes. Despite myself, I looked around to make sure the old cop's car was still a few yards away and he had not abandoned me to this cop and the forest and an unrequested sexcapade.

Now the cop managed to collect himself. He pulled his gaze from my shirt up to my eyes. Probably he was checking whether my pupils were dilated. All I could do was hope the pot had worn off enough by then to make my pupils normal size. I gazed right back into his dark eyes as if I had nothing to hide.

He nodded toward Tiffany in the car. "How much has she had to drink?"

"Give her a break, would you? I know she's blotto, but this is her first time drunk. Hell, it's her first drink. Drinks."

"Mmph," he said. Thank God he believed me. I might have gotten Tiffany off the hook. "And what about you?"

"Me?" I laughed. "I'm guilty."

He nodded. "What about the pot?"

I felt myself flash hot. Maybe he was bluffing. I asked, "What pot?"

The cop put his fists on his hips and cocked his head to one side. There probably was a line drawing of him like this in the dictionary, illustrating the word *skepticism.* "I might not have been to college," he said, "but I have been to the *police academy.*"

He pronounced *police academy* carefully, like it was a foreign word. I thought he was poking fun at himself. I almost laughed. I wasn't quite confident enough to laugh.

He went on, "What do you think we do at the *police academy,* surf the Internet?"

"I can honestly say I never gave it much th—"

"You know your boyfriend got expelled from Auburn for dealing pot out of his fraternity house," he said.

"That's why we're dating."

"You wanted some pot."

"Not so much that. It's just that Eric is my kind of people."

"Eric is—" He stopped himself with a grimace. Then he tried again. "You're an i—"

He was about to call me an idiot. Which I couldn't argue with, considering the present situation. But it was shocking to have a cop tell me so. Or almost tell me so. "I'm a what?" I taunted him.

He shook his head. "You can't tell a seventeen-year-old anything. They think they're immortal. They don't listen. Seventeen-year-olds have to see it for themselves."

"See what?"

He sighed through his nose. "Before I pulled y'all off the bridge, I glanced in your boyfriend's car. All I saw was two gallon jugs of beer. I don't have anything like possession on you. Come clean with me now, and maybe we won't do a drug screen on your boyfriend. You know if we do, we're charging him with driving under the influence of narcotics."

They certainly were. I backed against the cold car for strength and looked over at Eric's shoulders hunched into the other police car. Actually, I'd been dating him, if you could call it that, for only a few weeks. He had come home to live with his parents and "get his head together" (translation: "smoke a lot of weed") after the aforementioned untimely removal from the institution of higher learning.

But I knew him well enough to predict what his reaction would be. If I ratted on him and he got in trouble, he would call me a stupid bitch. If I didn't rat on him, they tested his piss, and he got in worse trouble, he would call me a stupid bitch.

"It was just me and him," I said in a rush. "Tiffany and Brian didn't know. They would have wigged out completely. We smoked it before we ran into them. Eric and I were baked and hungry, and we went to McDonald's for Big Macs. I saw Tiffany in the bathroom. I must have been obviously tanked, because Tiffany hinted she was going on the spring break senior trip next week without ever having a drink. She was afraid of looking naïve. And I'm like, 'Oh! Poor baby. I can buy you some beer.' Brian doesn't drink, either, but he went along with it. Probably for reasons you mentioned previously."

"Mmph," said the cop.

"It was a spur-of-the-moment thing. She never would have done it if she'd had time to think about it. And I never would have done it if I hadn't been stoned. Ditto walking onto the bridge. Completely unpremeditated."

I tried to gauge the cop's reaction. I couldn't see a thing. His dark eyes could have been laughing at me, or considering how I would look when I got out of prison just in time to join the AARP.

"Interesting," he said. "You've broken a lot of laws tonight."

Definitely laughing at me. I lashed out. "Let's list them, shall we? What fun. Trespassing. Possession of marijuana. Underage purchase of alcohol. What else? Public intoxication, loitering, unlawful assembly. Corruption of a minor. Wait, can you corrupt a minor when you yourself are also a minor?"

"You tell me. You're wearing the *Peer Pressure* T-shirt."

So he *had* noticed. "Yeah, I saw you taking in my *Peer Pressure* T-shirt," I said, just to test how *much* he'd noticed.

He'd noticed, all right. His white face and neck flushed pink against his dark blue uniform.

I was horrified, truly. I'd gathered over the years from the way men on TV talked about Taylor Swift and Miley Cyrus that forty-year-old men were really into teenage girls. I wouldn't have thought a blue-haired teenage girl would make the cut, but clearly there was no accounting for taste.

And here was this cop, out working hard at 11:30 at night, innocently providing for his wife and fourteen kids at home, scrimping and saving money for that new aluminum shed he'd had his eye on for storing the riding lawn mower. And I'd gone and flaunted my boobs in his face. It really wasn't his fault for looking.

He sighed through his nose again. His blush slowly retreated, and he was back in charge. "Are you even sorry?"

Yes, I was sorry for distracting him from the little missus for two seconds. Better not bring that up. "I'm sorry you arrested Tiffany. And maybe I'm sorry you arrested Brian." I was mad at Brian for abandoning Tiffany, but he *had* saved me from being handcuffed. Without the ulterior motive of getting himself out of more trouble, unlike Eric. "Do you want me to be sorry for getting stoned?"

"Are you sorry you almost got killed?"

"We didn't."

"You did!" Now he was furious, shouting down at me, finally giving me the Brian/Eric treatment. "Are you so drunk you didn't see that train?" He looked like he was going to lay into me again. I cringed, waiting for it.

But he thought better of it. His mouth snapped shut, and he took a step back.

Turning toward the bridge, he stared into the blackness. With my eyes adjusted to the pool of light from the cop cars, I couldn't even see past the *No Trespassing* sign. But the bridge had really made an impression on this cop. Seemed like he could see that bridge even in the dark.

3

The cop lightened up on the way to the police station. Or maybe it was just that the radio in the police car blasted Beck, which made the bad drug trip and forced incarceration a little more homey. I would have thought a cop would ride around in stark silence so nothing would distract him from his sworn duties. At the very least, I would have thought he'd listen to a country station. Maybe the last prisoner in the car had switched the radio to the Birmingham pop station as a joke.

Tiffany slouched against me, half asleep. Only the shoulder belt kept her from sagging into the floorboard. I was sleepy, too. The cop's interrogation had drained every drop of life out of me. And the drone of the car's engine lulled me. But I stayed in the middle of the seat. I tended to Tiffany, stroking her hair out of her eyes. This way, I could fool the cop, keeping the center seat belt lax across my lap without fastening it. I did not wear seat belts. Besides being a lot cheaper than a car, riding a motorcycle usually got me around this problem.

Tiffany shook her head and roused a little without opening her eyes. "Meg, you know what we are?"

"Criminals?" I guessed.

"Yes, but what else?"

"Felons?"

"We're no-goodniks!"

In the rearview mirror, I saw the cop smile. Obviously he liked Tiffany a lot better than he liked me.

She opened her eyes and saw him smiling, too. "Mr. Policeman, do you think we're no-goodniks?"

"Yes, but not for long."

"Well, I want you to know, for what it's worth, that I've learned my lesson. I have learned some things about myself tonight. They are all very bad."

I rubbed her thigh soothingly. I hadn't learned anything about myself tonight. I already knew these bad things.

"Your friend tells me this was your first drink," the cop said.

"Oh, no," she said.

"It *was* your first drink," I said through my teeth.

"I don't want to lie to the policeman." She sat up straighter. "Mr. Policeman, I went to England with my grandma last summer, and I had a can of shandy, which is beer mixed with lemonade. I bought it out of a Coke machine. My grandma said it was okay. Clearly it was wrong of her."

"Did you catch a buzz?" I asked.

"I don't know. I ate a lot of fish and chips with it."

The policeman laughed. Dimples showed in both his cheeks when he laughed.

I decided to try my hand at him. "Do you watch *Cops* on TV?"

"I love *Cops*," he said. "It's like my life, but with the boring parts taken out."

"Do you watch *Reno 911?*"

"Yes. That's probably even more true-to-life than *Cops*. At least around this town." He parked and cut the engine in front of the jail/courthouse/city hall, beside Tiffany's mom's minivan. "Sit tight just a minute, ladies." He slid out from under the steering wheel, closed the door, and spoke to the old cop through the rolled-down window of the other police car, with Brian and Eric in the backseat.

Eric said something to me through the glass. It did not look good. Then he struggled with his arms cuffed behind him. Finally his head and shoulders disappeared, and his cuffed hands rose above the windowsill. He shot me a bird.

I pointed out the spectacle to Tiffany. "I'm glad I'm not going to the prom. He might refuse to go with me now."

Tiffany rubbed her temple. "Invite him. We'll all double-date. Can you imagine where they would take us out to dinner?"

"McDonald's," I said with conviction as our cop opened the door.

The old cop was already hauling Brian and Eric out of his car. The message Eric had been trying to send me rang through the parking lot and echoed against the building. "You told him about the pot. He faked you out, you stupid bitch!"

"Well! That is not a very nice thing to say." I was actually kind of concerned about being faked out, and disappointed in myself. I had to keep up my rep around the Big House.

Our cop didn't even look at me. I was just another snitch to him. "Don't say anything else to each other," he intoned to the space between us.

"Pot?" Tiffany echoed behind me.

"Not you," our cop assured her. "I know you're not that much of a no-goodnik." He laughed and Tiffany giggled like they were old friends. God, these squares were *made* for each other.

Inside the police station, the cops didn't seem interested in fingerprinting us or taking our mug shots or dressing us in orange. Possibly this was because they didn't want to make a bigger scene. Tiffany's parents were already there to fuss over her hysterically. She clung to them like a terrified Pekingese who had gotten separated from her owners in a tornado. I had wondered why Tiffany didn't go Ivy League for college, with her grades and test scores. I sure would have gone farther than Birmingham if I'd gotten a scholarship somewhere else, somewhere that wasn't just another small town traded for this one. But after witnessing the collective fawning between Tiffany and her parents, I understood she wasn't ready to venture far.

"Call me tomorrow," she said as she left.

"I will," I said, knowing I wouldn't. I did not call people. Her parents took her home.

Brian's father arrived soon after. He was grim and quiet, like Brian. There was probably a lot of Silent Treatment going on in that household, and it probably worked. He took Brian home.

Then Eric's father blustered in. He acted like it was the policeman's fault for making the arrest, the city's fault for making the bridge off-limits, my fault for seducing his child. At least, I assumed he meant me when he said "that punk whore." He blamed anyone but Eric. He even dared to shout at my cop.

Not like the cop had shouted at Eric, right up in Eric's face. That was too personal. No, Eric's father paced around the cop and waved his arms, never looking directly into the cop's dark eyes. The cop stood there silently. He stared straight ahead like one of those soldiers on the Travel Channel who guarded the Tomb of the Unknown Soldier or Buckingham Palace with an expressionless face. He looked like he could use a shandy. Eric's father took Eric home.

Then the cop spent a long time on the phone in an office with a glass wall. I tried not to watch him, but he kept looking at me while he talked into the receiver. Probably he was telling his wife how much he loved her and how he would never cheat on her with a blue-haired girl-felon, if such a creature existed. After a long while, he hung up and returned to the main room, where he said something to the old cop that I couldn't quite catch. He leaned against the cement-block wall and folded his arms.

I yawned and stretched and shifted in my metal folding chair. I was watching an *Andy Griffith* rerun on the dispatcher's tiny TV. The dispatcher, whose name was Lois, had three grown children, eight grandchildren, two cats, two dogs, an iguana, lots of gold jewelry, and much bigger cleavage than mine. She lived at 2043 Sunny Level Cutoff and did not mind giving out her address to juvenile delinquents.

"Do you want to call your parents again?" the old cop asked me. His name was Officer Leroy. He had never married and did not have any children of his own, not even an iguana. "When I talked to your dad, he sounded like he was already awake."

Yes, my dad was already awake. My parents owned a diner called Eggstra! Eggstra! Underneath the name, the sign said *Our specialty is breakfast*, as if this were not painfully obvious already. It was open twenty-four hours a day, which is the only reason I could see that anyone would ever eat there.

"They're not coming," I said without looking up from the TV. I chuckled. This Barney Fife was a real laugh riot. I was still drunk.

"I'll try calling them." Officer Leroy picked up the phone on the dispatcher's desk.

"Please don't bother. This is the last straw," I repeated what my dad had said to me on the phone. "They've washed their hands of me."

In December when I skipped school with Davy Gillespie and Billy Smith and came home plastered, my dad had warned me this would happen. He'd told me that was my last time worrying my mother sick, and next time I would be dead to them. I hadn't exactly kept my nose clean since then. I'd done plenty with Eric. But I hadn't gotten caught, until now.

Officer Leroy put the phone down. Even though I still studied the exploits of Officer Barney Fife, I could feel Officer Leroy studying *me*. "I'm acquainted with your dad," he said finally. I got this a lot. Translation: *Your daddy is a hard-ass bastard.*

I snorted. "You played ball with him in school, right?"

"Seems you're his comeuppance." He slapped my cop on the shoulder and called a goodbye to Lois, who was speaking into her headset and typing at her computer. She waved back vaguely. Officer Leroy pushed open the door. Part of the cold night elbowed its way in as the door closed slowly behind him.

"Well, come on," my cop said to me. He shoved off the wall with one boot.

As I stood up to follow the cop, Lois called, "After." It seemed like she was talking to the cop. Yeah, I would have liked this tour of the jail *after*. After I was sober. After it was daylight. After I was sure I wouldn't have to spend the night here. But she heard something on her headphones, and her eyes glazed over. She spoke into her headset again and turned away.

The cop nodded a greeting to a guard watching his own TV, raked back a barred door, and led me down a cement-block hallway lined with jail cells. There were lots of sleepy catcalls, which I could handle. But one gentleman grabbed the bars of his cell, said, "Good evening, Clarice," and proceeded to list which of my body parts he planned to explore with his tongue. It took everything I had left in me to keep walking by him at the same slow pace.

"Shut up, Jerry," the cop said.

"Is this what you wanted me to see?" I asked the cop, trying to keep my shaking voice even.

"No, this is." The cop slid open an empty cell at the very end of the hall and motioned me in.

I stopped.

I breathed.

"Come on," he said.

I stepped toward him, stepped even with him, stepped past him into the cell, my heart pounding. I felt myself begin to panic. I whirled to face him and reached out with one hand to his shoulder. I didn't know what I was doing. I was just trying desperately to connect with him, like a friend, anything.

He started back. "Never touch me while I'm in uniform!" he shouted. The blush crept back into his white face. As if I were trying to come on to him and lead him astray from his wife and fourteen kids and storage shed, shiny and new from the Sears catalog.

"Okay," I whispered. I cradled the offending hand in the other hand and faced the far cement-block wall. The metal bars slid shut behind me with a *clang*. I tried to slow down my breathing. Red lights blinked behind my eyes, which was not a good sign. "Can you leave the door open a crack?"

"No."

"Can you leave it unlocked?"

"No."

"Can you put the key where I can reach it?"

"Like on *Andy Griffith?* That defeats the purpose of jail."

"Right." He was about to walk away. He was about to saunter back down the hall and leave me in this cell with two bunks secured to the wall with metal brackets, one metal toilet, and Hannibal Lecter next door. I couldn't slow down my breathing, and I could hardly see past the red blinking lights.

"Meg."

Creepy, this cop. "How do you know my name?"

"I'm well acquainted with your driver's license. I've pulled you over twice in the past few months for riding your motorcycle without a helmet."

Oh *yeah*. Now I vaguely remembered this asshole. But—and it was amazing that my brain could process this in its current state—my driver's license listed my name as Margaret, not Meg. Somehow he knew I was Meg and not one of the other nicknames for Margaret, all of which I'd been called by my elderly relatives when I was little. "How do you know I'm not Maggie?" I asked the cement-block wall. "Peg? Margot? Of course, Margot has always reminded me of a fungus." I was panting.

"Meg, look at me."

I began to turn. As I shifted my head, the darkness closed in. The cop appeared through the bars at the end of a long tunnel that collapsed as I watched.

MY SKIN SHRANK AGAINST MY BONES. I could feel myself shrinking and floating up.

ONE MORE NOSE FULL OF AMMONIA and I knocked the smelling salts away with my hand. The cold of Lois's metal desktop soaked through to my shoulder blades. I turned away from the close-up of her Rolodex and faced the cop's belt buckle. He pressed two fingers to the inside of my wrist and looked at his watch, checking my pulse.

I reviewed what must have happened. I fainted on the floor of the jail cell. Ew. And the cop picked me up in his big strong arms and carried me here.

Ew?

"She's faking," the cop said, hating me with his dark eyes. "She made herself pass out by hyperventilating."

Yes, ew.

"It doesn't matter whether she's faking or not," Lois called from somewhere across the room. "Most high school girls would get upset if you threw them in the pen with a bunch of men."

"There were no men in the cell with her."

"Would you give it a rest, After?" Lois said.

"Better yet," I said weakly, "give it a rest right now."

The cop removed his fingers from my wrist. "Do you have any medical conditions we should know about?" he asked me in his Official Capacity.

"Do I? What year is this?" I remembered running five miles that morning. "No, not today." I sat up slowly on the desk.

"Here, sweetie." Lois handed me a Sprite. I popped the top with tingling fingers and took one gulp.

"Drink faster," the cop said. "You can't have food or beverage in the cell."

"You are *not* going to put her back in there," Lois said in disbelief.

"Lois, I didn't pick her up for jaywalking. You're going to let her spend the night sipping Sprite and watching TV?"

"The other three are spending the night at home with their mamas, in bed."

They stared each other down for a few seconds.

"Shouldn't you be on patrol?" Lois hinted.

The cop cussed, stalked across the room, and flung open the door. This time an even larger piece of the cold night stepped inside as the door closed very slowly. He was gone.

"Thank you," I sighed.

"Mmmm-hmmm." Lois helped me down from the desk and back to my metal folding chair. She sat down, too, and spoke softly into her headset.

When she stopped talking and looked at me again, I asked, "What's his problem?"

"He's a good cop," she said. "A little too good, maybe."

"What's so good about him? He harassed me." I set down my Sprite and put my head in my hands. "If this town ain't big enough for the two of us, I'll be gone to Birmingham soon. All I want is to graduate in June. And go to Miami next week."

She murmured into the headset. Then she asked, "Miami? What for? Spring break?"

"Yeah," I said dreamily.

"With your folks?"

"No, thank God. Tiffany and Brian and I are going with

a bunch of seniors from school. It's chaperoned, but loosely. Everybody wants to go on this trip. Each year, the football coach gets the cheerleading sponsor drunk on the first night, and nobody hears from them again until the end of the week. It's a tradition."

Lois slumped a little in her chair. "I hate to be the one to break this to you, sweetie."

"Break *what* to me?" As if spending the night in the police station was too good to be true.

"I hope you don't think the officer who arrested you is through with you. I overheard him on the phone with the Powers That Be a little while ago. He's got your number."

"He's got my number?" Did she mean my phone number? He was planning to call me, despite his wife and fourteen children and the storage shed? He must be going through a midlife crisis.

"He's hitting you where it hurts," Lois said. "He wants to make sure you kids don't get out of these charges with your parents paying a fine. He wants *you* to pay. But he wants you rehabilitated, not sent to juvy. So he came up with a plan."

"I hate plans."

"One of you will spend a week riding with the fire truck, one with the ambulance, and one with the police patrol. All the people you dragged out to the railroad bridge in the middle of the night."

"What about the fourth one of us?" I asked, knowing the answer already.

She rolled her eyes. "I think everyone assumes that lawyer will get his druggie son off, like he always does."

Of course.

"And by the end of the week," she said, "you'll have to turn in a proposal to the Powers That Be for a project to discourage other kids from doing what you did."

God, how Goody Two-shoes. But I was sure I could bullshit my way through this stupid proposal in my sleep. "It doesn't sound too bad. The riding around part actually sounds like fun. Maybe they'll let me drive." It probably *would* sound like fun if I didn't feel right now like I'd been run over by that train.

"They want you to do it during the night shift," she said.

"I can handle that."

She shook her head sadly. "They want you to do it during your spring break, so you can spend a week on night shift without missing school."

It took a second to sink in. Then I screamed, "What? That cop is the Devil!"

"No, he just understands how teenagers think."

I wasn't sure this was true. The cop thought I had plans to spend my spring break getting drunk and showing off my tits. Yes, there was that. But there was more. I felt tears well up in my eyes as I pictured the vast blue Atlantic. My parents used to talk about taking me to Florida someday when they'd saved up money. That talk stopped a few years ago. Now I'd spent my entire life five hours from the beach without ever seeing the ocean.

My first thought was for myself, of course. But my next thought was for my mom. While someone else supposedly chaperoned me in Miami, my parents were planning to take their first vacation in four years, to Graceland. They could still go while I served my time on night shift. Anyone else's parents would go. But I knew my mom. She would stay home now. Hell, she'd ride with me in the cop car if they let her. She would cancel her vacation because of me, and I would suffer the Punishment Worse Than Jail: guilt. It was enough to drive a girl to drink. Again.

"I know it seems like the end of the world to you," Lois said, patting my knee. "That's exactly what he was counting on. But an adult can see that you are very, very, very lucky, and you should be grateful. Isn't this better than going to court?"

I considered this question. Bad things could happen at court. Probably I wouldn't get locked up, but there was an outside chance. I shivered and pulled my jacket closer around me.

If I got to ride in the ambulance, it might be better than going to court. I did not like ambulances, and I liked being closed into them even less. But Quincy, my paramedic friend, would ride with me. He understood my problem and could help me out. He'd been an ass to me at the bridge, but I figured he'd been putting on a Disapproving Adult act in front of the other Disapproving Adults.

Riding on the fire engine would be even better. I'd get a lot of sleep. There wasn't much to this town, so there wasn't much to catch on fire. Definitely better than going to court.

But I might have to ride with the cops. Specifically, my cop. In that case, I wasn't so sure it was worth it.

4

Lois got off work at 6 A.M. and offered to take me home. She said I was supposed to stay in jail until my parents came to sign me out. But when I told her if they hadn't shown up by now, they wouldn't be here until the lunch crowd thinned out, she said screw that. Her exact words were, "Screw that. I'll take you on home, hon."

Like any fifty-year-old who had a little money saved up and considered herself a free spirit, Lois drove a VW Bug with a yellow faux flower in the dashboard bud vase to match the yellow paint job. As we stopped at the edge of the jail/courthouse/city hall parking lot to turn onto the highway, a police car pulled in. Out of the corner of my eye I saw the cop raise his hand in greeting to Lois—and then he *erked* to a stop half in the parking lot, half on the highway. Yes, it was my cop. I wouldn't have thought he would notice me in the passenger side of Lois's car with the streetlights glinting off the windshield. However, I did have blue hair, which was like walking around with a Sims arrow over my head.

He rolled down his window and scowled at Lois, willing her to roll down her window, too. Uh-oh. He would call her out for transporting a hardened criminal without authorization. He would take me back inside. My heart pounded and my body braced for another blow from this man who'd decided I needed a nemesis, as if I didn't get enough of that from my dad already.

Lois floored it. The g-force pressed me back against the seat as the Bug tore onto the highway. The little engine whined in protest. "Give it a rest, Officer After," Lois muttered. "I'll put you over my knee and spank your bottom."

I turned to stare at her in surprise.

She glanced nervously over at me. "What."

"Nothing." I didn't want to admit I'd been too drunk to figure out the cop's name until now. And since she was nice enough to drive me home, it seemed rude to broach the subject of sexual relations during the graveyard shift at the police department. If she wanted to engage in extramarital spanking with a man ten years her junior, well, that was between her and Officer After and his wife and fourteen kids and Lois's iguana, et cetera. Though I seriously doubted that Lois—or anyone else—ever inflicted corporal punishment on Officer After. The whole way home she checked her mirrors, expecting blue lights to burst on behind us. But he had let us go.

She pulled into the diner parking lot. Gravel popped beneath the tires. Wiping his hands on a rag, my dad glowered out at me from behind the counter. Then he turned back to the grill.

"I don't want to see any more of you," Lois told me, "at least until next weekend. Keep your nose clean." She tapped the tip of her nose twice. Some of her heavy makeup had rubbed off overnight. Red veins showed through.

Yes ma'am, I will, would have been the polite thing to say. But I did not make promises. "Thanks for everything."

Instead of the diner, I headed for the trailer. It had come with the diner. My parents had decided we would live in it temporarily to save money until the diner got established as the town's premier eatery and they could afford to build their dream home. We lived here still.

The whole thing shook when I slammed the metal door behind me. The floor creaked as I walked to the bathroom. After my fainting spell in the jail, my body wanted to go for a jog and prove to me that it was not sick, it was not wasting away, it was okay. But my head throbbed. I needed more time to recover from the beer. And I was scheduled to work all morning. Something in my dad's glower had told me I'd better not use jail time as an excuse to skip out of work. I could jog later. I showered with the curtain open, mopped up the water on the floor with a towel. Then I slipped on a low-cut shirt that seemed inappropriate for work, yet 50 percent less inflammatory than my *Peer Pressure* T-shirt under the circumstances, and went to face the music.

I made my entrance through the front door so I could bus dishes and greet my dad with my arms already full. My mom sat in a booth with a couple of regulars, probably complaining to them about what I'd done now. She looked like the *before* on one of those TV makeover shows. Bad perm. Forty pounds overweight. Enormous T-shirt with a picture of a kitten, paws on its head, and a thought balloon: "Is it the weekend yet?" Which made absolutely no sense because both my parents worked through the weekend. We all did.

When my mom saw me, she opened her mouth. Her eyes darted to my dad behind the counter. She closed her mouth and watched me with a tortured expression as I passed. I knew my dad had coached her: *When Meg comes in, don't you go over there and hug on her like she won a beauty contest.*

Without a word to anyone, I stacked dishes into the washer, tied on my apron, and took customers' orders. I waitressed and cooked, cleaning each little mess before my dad could point it out to me. If I worked fast enough, adrenaline put up a wall between me and my throbbing headache.

I was chopping sausage and reliving my jail time, wishing I knew exactly where Officer After had put his hands as he picked me up off the floor so I could turn the tables and get him in trouble with the Powers That Be, when my dad grumbled from the grill, "You've got a lot of nerve to come back here."

His beard hid his chin, so I couldn't tell anything from the set of his jaw. But his blue eyes snapped at the eggs on the grill. This was new territory. He might have washed his hands of me, but he'd never suggested I couldn't come home. Until now.

Normally the implied threat would have scared me silent. But

Officer After had shocked the life out of me quite a few times over the course of the night, and I'd had enough. I banged the knife down on the cutting board beside the sausage. "Oh, you're kicking me out of the 'house'?" I made finger quotes. "And you're 'firing' me?" My parents made me work, but they didn't pay me. I reminded them of this whenever I got in trouble. "Good luck getting Bonita to cover my shift. She keeps her grandkids in the mornings."

He glanced up to make sure my mom was on the other end of the kitchen, out of earshot. Then he hissed, "I don't give a shit what your mother says. I'm tired of you playing her like a piano. I'm taking her to Graceland like we planned."

"You—" I stopped short. There was no point in whispering, *You're sending me to juvy?* He would say I'd sent myself. Just then my mother dropped a baking pan with a *clang* like the jail cell door closing. The blood drained from my face and pooled around my feet. My heart sped up, pumping nothing. But I would not let my dad see me faint over this. I leaned farther forward over the counter and chopped more sausage, wondering vaguely where the knife would cut me when I lost consciousness.

My dad growled at me, "*You* are going to spend your spring break pulling night shift with that cop After, like the DA said on the phone. And then you're going to work morning shift here. If you have the energy to get yourself arrested in the eight hours you have left in the day . . ." Expertly he slid his spatula under the eggs and flipped them to cook on the other side without breaking the yolks. "*Vaya con Dios.*"

I watched the eggs sizzling on the grill, the yolks slowly

growing darker. "What do you mean, I'm pulling night shift with After? I thought I might be on the fire truck or the ambulance."

"That's not what the DA said." My dad turned to me for the first time, blue eyes hot with fury. "You think you've got some more to learn riding in the ambulance?"

"Been there, done that," I sang, using the knife to scrape the sausage from the cutting board into a bowl. I pretended to put together the rest of the hash brown casserole with busy efficiency like I was kicking ass on *Iron Chef*. But I was thinking of Officer After, his dark eyes sliding to my cleavage, his phantom hands on my helpless body. Now that I knew about my punishment, I rather liked the idea of taunting him with my sexy if by some chance we happened to be paired together. Screw his wife.

But if he'd not only masterminded the demise of my spring break but also *chosen* me to spend it with, he was back in control. Maybe he even intended to have his way with me. Stranger things had happened. More horrible things.

And I would deserve it.

"You stay in the vehicle," Officer After commanded me. "I may have to draw my weapon."

I frowned across the front seat at him. I had thought he might make me sit in the backseat tonight. Glory be, I had graduated to the front. And he didn't have a military haircut anymore. In the week since our unfortunate meeting, it had filled out into an almost normal haircut. He no longer looked like he'd just gotten back from Iraq.

Then I glanced at the rusty Caddy ahead of us on the shoulder of the highway, awash in broad strokes of blue from the police car lights. "Your weapon? Do you mean your gun? Why? They were just speeding."

"You haven't seen what I've seen. Yet." He used the controls in his door to raise my window, which I'd kept down all night despite the cold.

"Part of my assignment is to go with you everywhere and find out what your job is really like. I can't do that from the car."

"I think there's a rule that when my weapon comes out, you stay in the vehicle."

"No rule like that was specified by the Powers That Be."

He sighed through his nose. "If you get wounded, I'm pretty sure I'll be reassigned to jail guard duty."

"I won't get wounded."

"I'm not going to argue with you. Do what I say." He opened the door.

"Wait a minute," I said, putting one hand on his bare forearm.

He looked down at my hand. *Don't touch me while I'm in uniform.* So much for his wanting to have his way with me.

I snatched my hand away. "Sorry. Reflex. But look, you can't leave me locked in your car. What if *you* get shot and I'm stuck in here?"

I didn't believe he'd get shot. I didn't believe *anyone* would get shot. Not considering how we'd spent tonight's patrol. After all his tough talk when he arrested me about how he wanted me to *see something*, this is what I had seen: I had seen a city cop herding cows out of the mayor's strawberry fields and back into the pasture next door. And I was paying this cop's salary with my tax dollars. Or I would be, if I were paying taxes, if I worked a paying job instead of slaving without pay at the diner. I owed, like, a dollar every year in taxes on my tips.

We had harassed a lot of innocent people. We chased skateboarders away from the sidewalks in the roundabout in the center of town. We chased kids parked in pickup trucks away from the back of the movie theater. Lois was right when she said Officer After knew how teenagers thought. Sneaky shit.

We had worked a fender bender at the Birmingham Junction, the intersection of the highway through town and the interstate to Birmingham. The Birmingham Junction was famous for wrecks, but this one wasn't even interesting—just a shattered taillight and a couple of infuriatingly polite Japanese businessmen from the car factory.

We had driven down to the bridge with the headlights off three or four times to make sure kids weren't drinking there. Ides of March, my ass. It wasn't bad luck Officer After had caught us at the bridge. He caught us because he haunted that bridge, just as if he were the ghost of someone who'd died there himself.

We had eaten dinner, or whatever you called the 1 A.M. meal, at Eggstra! Eggstra! I could tell Officer After did this every night. Purcell served him coffee and cooked for him without asking for

44

his order, just like he did for me. Weird that this had been going on in my backyard and I didn't even know, because I usually got off work around ten. While Officer After and I ate, the diner got slammed with the crowd heading home from the demolition derby. Of course Purcell wanted me to take orders and serve drinks while he cooked, and of course I refused. It was bad enough that my parents didn't pay me for working there. I sure as hell wasn't going to work there for free when it wasn't even my shift.

Purcell actually had the nerve to start cussing at me. I guess he wasn't worried about his job security. Our town offered plenty of jobs for an illiterate, and most of them probably paid better.

He cussed at me, that is, until Officer After half stood. That's all it took. Purcell suddenly became engrossed in flipping the chopped steak on the grill. Officer After went back to eating like nothing had happened, without looking at me.

Without talking to me, either. We'd spent most of the night in silence. And when we parked by the highway, cut the lights, and waited for speeders, it was like a game of sleep-chicken. Who would snore first?

It was torture. I had gotten off work at Eggstra! Eggstra! that afternoon, gone for my jog, and then tried my best to sleep, but come on. I never slept at 3 P.M. And I was too keyed up about tonight. Now Officer After was making me pay. Wasn't it enough to miss spring break of my senior year in high school so I could ride around this town with a cop all night? He didn't have to bore me to death, too.

No chance of that now.

"You'll still be able to get out the door," he said. "I've set it so only the back doors are locked and suspects can't get out. And no one will be able to open your door from the outside. Suspects can't get in."

"Get *in?*" I echoed as he hauled himself out of the seat with lots of *clicks* and *clanks* from the equipment attached to his belt and closed the heavy door behind him with an official-sounding *thunk*. But he was bluffing, trying to scare me. The blue lights took swipes at the back of his uniform as he walked casually to the rusty Caddy and stopped just behind the driver's door. He bent to talk to the driver through the window.

And then he slowly reached back with one hand and unsnapped his gun holster.

Frantically I felt for my cell phone in my pocket. I did not call people, but I pressed the button to call Tiffany at the hospital. We weren't close like we were as kids. We were back to being the tentative friends we'd been since eighth grade. Or maybe a little less, now that I'd caused her to miss her spring break and lose her boyfriend. But at school on Friday, I'd traded cell phone numbers with her when she asked. She'd told me the paramedics watched TV or slept at the hospital most of the night. But they'd warned her that when they did get a call, all hell would break loose. She'd wanted someone she could call to save her in case the speeding ambulance turned over. This was a similar emergency.

"Hello?" she said sleepily.

"Wake up," I hissed. "It's Meg. I need you to be on 911 alert. If I scream, bring the paramedics to the highway between the Shop

Till You Drop convenience store and the Golden Cherry Motel. The cop has his hand on his gun."

"He has his hand on his gun?" She was awake now.

"I thought it was just a traffic stop. He has his hand on his gun. I'm sure there's some way for me to alert Lois the dispatcher from inside the police car, but there's not a red button clearly labeled *Call for Help*." I let out a little whimper and wanted to kick myself.

"What's he doing?"

"Standing beside the car, talking to the driver."

"Calm down, Meg. He radioed in about what he was doing, right? And if he wanted backup, they're on the way."

"But what if they're across town? And what if he gets gunned down on the highway? I would feel so much better knowing the ambulance was already headed over here. Oh God, why didn't I pay more attention to Resusci-Annie in health class? Never mind, I'll tell you why not. It was Derek Bledsoe's turn to resuscitate her before me, and he slobbered all over her. Somehow the fresh sheet of Saran Wrap over her mouth did not make me feel protected."

"Meg, would you calm down? I've never heard you this upset. Nothing upsets you. Except, you know, claustrophobia."

"Now he's dragging the driver out of the car, handcuffing him, searching him."

"Calm down. Get your mind off it." She paused. "Was your dad right about this policeman being the one from the bridge?"

"Yeah."

"Is he cute?"

Strangely, I felt myself blush. At least she *was* getting my mind off his imminent death. "You saw him that night."

"I told you at school. The only thing I remember from that night is babbling something about shandy and trying to blame it all on my grandmother."

"Right. Well, he has these beautiful dark brown eyes, sleepy eyes that look you over slowly."

"Oh!"

"But other than that, he's military cop guy. You know, perfectly pressed uniform, shiny boots."

"Oh." She sounded disappointed. Then she lowered her voice to a whisper. "Be glad you don't have to spend spring break with *these* people."

"I *have* spent a lot of time with one of them, Quincy with the gray hair. He usually took me in the ambulance to the hospital in Birmingham."

"Really? Well, they are full of stories now. They say almost every household accident they get called to involves alcohol. Or a chain saw."

"Or alcohol *and* a chain saw."

"I see you've heard these stories. I'm like, people, I'm going to be an English major, not a doctor. And I'm never drinking again. So you really could skip it."

"It will pass, and they'll move on to the fireworks stories. At least you're getting some sleep."

She yawned. "You still haven't heard from Eric?"

"No." I *would* hear from him, though. He'd be furious with me right up until he was ready to make a booty call. That's how Eric worked. "And you still haven't heard from Brian? You haven't gone on an ambulance run and seen him on the fire truck?"

"No." She sounded forlorn. Brian had refused to speak to either of us at school last week. He acted like a martyr enduring trial by fire rather than a high school senior getting ribbed about his arrest.

Tiffany didn't remember anything from that night. So she didn't remember that when the long arm of the law reached out and grabbed Brian off the bridge, Brian abandoned her. But she probably didn't want to know. She and I were in very different places when it came to boys. She wanted a relationship, and I wanted a lay.

"What's your cop's name?" she asked. "You said he seemed to know us at the bridge. Did he turn out to be someone's dad?"

"I don't know. His name is Officer After."

"*After*, as in *before?*"

"Yeah. In fact, I asked him if Barry B. Four was his maternal grandfather, and he didn't laugh. Then I asked him what he was after. He said he could tell me but he'd have to kill me."

"I think I know who that is, Meg. What's his first name?"

"As far as I know, Officer."

"Is he tall?"

"Not as tall as Eric."

"Nobody's as tall as Eric," she said. "Thin?"

I gazed ahead at his Matt Damon body. "Oh, no."

"Blond?"

"I honestly couldn't say. His hair is one-half of an inch long."

"Meg, I know who that is. It's—"

5

Oh shit!" I squeaked. The passenger of the Caddy opened his door and dashed into the woods. Officer After called to him, drew his weapon, and aimed briefly. Then he swore, holstered the gun, and took off after the suspect.

"What happened?" Tiffany asked sharply. "The paramedics have been listening to Officer After on the scanner. Another policeman is on the way."

"Tell him to hurry." The driver, handcuffed and leaning against the Caddy, had seen me. He walked toward the police car, shouting things at me that I did not want to hear.

"Who is that?" Tiffany asked. "Surely he's not saying that to *you?* Where is his mother?"

He came closer. "Tiffany," I said, "Officer After is in hot pursuit of another suspect." The driver reached the front bumper of the police car. "I do not feel safe." He reached my door and gave it a solid kick. The whole car shook. I backed over the siren controls and into Officer After's seat. "I am full of fear."

There was a shout outside the car, and a flash of nightstick. The back door opened. Officer After shoved the driver into the backseat. Then came the passenger, simultaneously gasping for breath and moaning.

And that was that.

Officer After slammed the door and walked around the car. I slid to my side of the seat and reached for my door handle to escape from this jail containing other criminals. But Officer After opened his own door and squeezed himself under the steering wheel.

Now I felt safe.

Another cop car pulled up, blue lights whirling. Officer Leroy walked past us and peered into the Caddy with a flashlight.

From behind me, the driver suspect yelled at Officer Leroy, as if Officer Leroy could hear him. The passenger suspect continued to moan. Officer After shouted a few words into his CB at Lois. Then he turned up the Birmingham rock station on the back speakers. This drowned out the suspects with a rap about smoking pot. It did not seem to be an effective way to kick off the suspects' rehabilitation, much less mine.

Officer After was oblivious. Years as a cop must have taught him to tune things out. He reached for his clipboard and began filling out forms. A vein throbbed in his neck, but he was hardly winded.

"So, nice chatting with you, Tiff," I chirped into the phone.

"No problem," Tiffany said weakly. "Good night."

I clicked the phone off and stuffed it into my pocket, then reached down to the floorboard for my notebook. I had told Officer After I needed to take notes for my bullshit Goody Two-shoes proposal for the Powers That Be. Really I just wanted something to do while he crossed out forms on his clipboard in that annoying Official Manner he had.

I had already written *Ides of March*, *police academy*, *get in your pants*, and *something I want you to see*. Now I added *vehicle*, *draw weapon*, *wounded*, and *suspect*. Still scribbling, I asked Officer After offhandedly, "What was so dangerous about that? Herding cows was more dangerous."

"Don't laugh," he said. "Herding cows really can be dangerous. You don't want it to be exciting. You're lucky there wasn't a bull." He drew an *X* through a section of the form. "Chickens are also difficult." His dimples showed again when he laughed, just like he'd laughed for Tiffany that first night. He still wasn't laughing for me. He was laughing at his own joke. Aw, Hulk Hogan made a funny.

The passenger suspect kept moaning, and the driver suspect yelled more loudly at Officer Leroy. Without turning around, Officer After said, "Shut up, Zeke. Hang in there, Demetrius," and turned up the radio again—All-American Rejects, "Dirty Little Secret." He went back to his forms. I studied him as he wrote.

I wondered if I was developing Stockholm Syndrome, identifying with my captor like Elizabeth Smart. Or if I was having some preprogrammed biological cavewoman reaction to a caveman saving me from a saber-toothed tiger. Because at the bridge when he threatened me, I'd only noticed Officer After's dark uniform, white face, dark eyes. And his dimples. Now that he'd rescued me, so to speak, I noticed a lot more.

I noticed how smooth his face was, except for a scruff of five o'clock shadow (in this case, a bit after 5 A.M.) and some worry lines between his eyebrows. I noticed how sensitive and soft his mouth looked as he bit his lip gently, considering a section of the form. I noticed how long his blond eyelashes were, fringing his dark eyes. His lashes were not stubbly. This certified he had cut the hair on his head so short on purpose. He was not growing it back after losing it all to chemotherapy.

I'd never been attracted to older guys, my friends' fat dads. I had even wondered how their wives could stand to have sex with them. But with Officer After, it was strange. I could sort of see how it wouldn't feel like hell on earth to be his wife.

He probably got her pregnant when they were both a little older than me, maybe nineteen like my parents had been. Now Officer After had four children (down from fourteen—he seemed more responsible than *that*), with the oldest about to finish high school and get pregnant herself.

They lived in a triple-wide trailer and were very happy. His wife stayed up some nights, listening to the police scanner just to feel close to him. There was a lot of warm fruit cobbler. She cooked with butter, and this was one of the things that made him horny for her after all these years.

She went easy on the fruit cobbler herself so she could keep her girlish figure. She was one of the women around this town who looked like a hick but very, very pretty and carefully kept up if you could see past the big hair. Like Lois, twenty years ago. Oh, yeah, she turned Officer After *on*.

Unlike me. I glanced down at my shirt. No cleavage tonight. Though I'd fantasized about it a little, in the end the whole seducing-a-married-man thing had made even *me* uncomfortable. Tonight I was wearing a crew-neck skull-and-crossbones T-shirt to get across how I felt about my punishment, in case this was not already clear.

"I don't think you were worried about the danger to me," I said. "I think you wanted me to stay in the car because you were embarrassed to be seen with me in front of the suspects."

He looked up from his forms at me. Then he peered through the metal grate at the suspects. Demetrius was still moaning. Zeke snarled, "What're *you* looking at?"

"You have the right to remain silent," Officer After told Zeke. He looked at me. "I don't know what you mean. Why would I be embarrassed to be seen with you?"

He asked so earnestly that I felt like I had to explain the obvious. "My hair, and the way I dress."

"You dress like you're Japanese," he said.

"The clueless Japanese who work at the car factory and wear those weird plastic sandals? Thanks."

"No, the cute Japanese girls you see at the mall in Birmingham."

He looked down at his forms, pen poised. But he didn't write anything. That blush crept up from his neck and across his cheeks. He had just realized he'd called me cute.

"I mean, the Japanese girls," he said, still looking down. "You know how you dress. With your T-shirt and your jacket and your jeans and your shoes and your weird socks and your hairpins and your blue hair."

He was digging himself a deeper hole. Now he had told me he'd noticed every detail of what I looked like. Maybe that was part of his police training, so he could provide an accurate description of me when I escaped. Although *blue hair* probably would be sufficient to get me picked up.

Or maybe he was attracted to me.

I watched as he drew an *X* on the form and brusquely flipped to another page. I honestly didn't know what to think anymore. Usually I was very good at reading people. I didn't get emotionally involved. When you were an outsider looking in, it was easy to see clearly. This guy I couldn't read.

"You dress like a manga character," he said.

Well, that explained everything. "Your kids read manga?" He probably had a daughter into manga, and I reminded him of his daughter. He had blushed because he thought I'd gotten the wrong idea. And he was right.

Now he looked up at me and held his hands out flat, pen between two fingers. "What kids?"

I noticed his left hand was bare. "They don't let you wear your wedding ring on the job?"

He turned his big hand over and looked at it. "What wedding ring? I'm not married."

Zeke told me I could come to his prison for a conjugal visit any time I wanted. He would tie me down. My heart sped up like he really was tying me down with his words. *Bitch* encircled one of my wrists, *cock* held the other, and *spread* was snaking around my left ankle.

I dumped my notebook out of my lap and tried the door handle. Locked. "Shit." I pounded the window. "Let me out, God damn it!"

I heard the lock slide open. Then I tried the handle again, bailed out onto the grassy shoulder, and jogged toward the Caddy, away from the *heh heh heh* of Zeke.

Beyond the pool of headlights and the sweep of blue lights, the night was black. The highway was empty. Officer Leroy bent over in the Caddy, peering under the seats. I guess it was because he knew my dad (even if he didn't *like* my dad), but I thought he would protect me from the suspects. And Officer After. Funny how a near-stranger's weighty ass provided me comfort.

But I couldn't really feel comfortable while a low hum vibrated through me. I looked around nervously until I realized it was Officer Leroy's car engine on idle.

Officer After lit a cigarette behind his door, out of the wind. Then he tossed the pack into the car, closed the door, and walked toward me. He settled next to me, half sitting on the bumper of the Caddy.

I scooted a little farther away from him. "You promised me you wouldn't lock me in the car."

He exhaled smoke. "I didn't lock you in before. I locked it when I got back in. I forgot. Habit."

"Still. Your idea of punishing me is to stand me up in a corner and let lecherous men call me names."

"I hadn't thought about it like that. But it's fitting, in a way." He gestured with the cigarette, trailing smoke and a spot of fire. "It's a warning about the kind of people you'll meet if you keep doing pot after Eric is found facedown, dead in a ditch in a few years, and your ready supply runs out. The suspect who was impolite to you at the city jail last week is waiting to be transferred to the state pen on narcotics charges. And we're going to find something good in here." He patted the trunk of the Caddy. "We catch a lot of folks running drugs from Florida through here to Birmingham. They assume they're safe if they're off the interstate. They're wrong."

"I hate to tell you this," I said, "but drug runners don't stash their pot in the trunk like a suitcase or a spare tire."

"Yes, they do. There's no way to hide it anyway once we get the dog out here. They know that. They just hope this won't be the time they get caught. But they're high themselves, and they have poor judgment. They don't understand they could greatly reduce their chances of getting caught by driving the speed limit. And by choosing a vehicle other than a stolen 1987 Cadillac Eldorado." He tapped ash onto the asphalt and took another drag. Exhaling, he said, "It's cold out here. Come back to the car. We'll leave as soon as Leroy finishes his search."

"I'll come back to the car after you put that out. I don't want to breathe your secondhand smoke. Talk about a dangerous job."

He laughed shortly. "Pot's a lot more carcinogenic than cigarettes."

"And if I were a complete pothead, which I'm not, I still wouldn't be smoking the equivalent of a pack a day."

"I don't smoke that much, either."

True. This was the first cigarette he'd smoked in the nearly eight hours I'd spent with him on his shift. His habit couldn't have been too intense.

"You will, though," I said. "It's addictive. It's like trapping yourself."

Eyeing me, he took an especially long drag. Like he was flaunting it, *so there*. This reaction seemed immature of him. I wondered how old he was, since he didn't have a wife and kids. The short hair, big muscles, and official uniform made him seem older than he probably was. The way he moved and spoke with such confidence.

He flicked away the cigarette butt (littering wasn't a crime suddenly?) and nodded toward the car. I hauled open my heavy door emblazoned with the city seal and the police department motto, *To Protect and Serve*, and sat down on the vinyl. The radio blasted Mariah Carey's "Touch My Body."

Shouting over the music, Zeke gave me a few details about how he was going to rape me.

Officer After leaned across the seat toward me—which, under the circumstances, made me start back. "I'm sorry I'm not allowed to beat the shit out of him for you."

"Oh, that's quite all right."

"It's one of the first things they teach you at the *police academy*." Officer After turned to Zeke. "Say one more thing to her and I'll add corruption of a minor to the list of charges." Then he whispered to me, "I'm glad you reminded me of that one last weekend. Handy."

"Aw, man!" Zeke said. "This is the last female I'm going to get for about two years."

"You're not *getting* this one." Through the window, Officer After made a super-secret cop motion. Officer Leroy waddled over and dragged Zeke out of the backseat. Stumbling after Officer Leroy on the way to the other cop car, Zeke looked back at me and licked his lips.

"Ready?" Officer After asked me. I nodded. I was relieved Zeke was gone, but the weight of what he'd said to me still sat on my lungs. Demetrius's tortured moans from the backseat were a constant reminder.

"Put your seat belt on," Officer After said impatiently. "I don't want to have this conversation with you every time I start the vehicle."

I waited, hoping he would start the car anyway. He didn't. "I can't," I said.

"You can. I didn't say anything the night I arrested you, when you pretended to wear it. You were in the backseat where it's safer, and I was tired of arguing with you. But police cars won't start unless the front seat belts are fastened."

I glared at him. "Do you think I'm a crack ho? How stupid do you think I am?"

"Then let me put it to you this way. Either fasten your seat belt, or we go to the police station right now, call the DA, and tell her the deal's off."

The seat belt felt like a hairy arm as I pulled it across my chest, and the click as I fastened it sounded like a key in a lock.

Officer After cranked the engine and pulled onto the highway. We sat in silence for a few minutes, except for the radio, Demetrius's moaning, and my own breathing in my ears.

Finally Officer After said, "Meg."

He probably realized I was going to faint again. My arms were crossed. I'd learned in public-speaking class at school that this position told people you felt uncomfortable. As if I could have hidden this. It also pushed my breasts up so I looked like I had a more ample bosom. In addition, my chest heaved with heavy breathing. My skull-and-crossbones T-shirt looked like a pirate flag waving in the breeze. No wonder Officer After had noticed.

"Meg, I'm sorry," he said. "It's illegal in Alabama to drive without a seat belt. I can't have you doing something illegal in my police car."

It was touching for him to be so sweet to a criminal. I felt halfway guilty about making him feel bad. It really wasn't his fault.

However, as I was having some trouble staying conscious, I concentrated on my own needs. I hit the button to roll down the window and hung my head out like a dog. Between moans, Demetrius complained about the wind and the cold. But unlike Zeke, he didn't mention my privates, so he was easier to ignore.

Watching the sickeningly familiar highway and trees and

buildings spin by, I wondered whether Graceland was everything my mom had dreamed or if she was actually more impressed by the chandelier in the lobby of Memphis's Comfort Inn.

I wondered whether the football coach, the cheerleading sponsor, and my classmates had reached Miami in the bus yet. I wondered if they would get drunk first thing, or if they would run down to the beach first, like I would have done. I wondered how the sand felt between their toes, and whether the water was soft and warm.

I sat up when we pulled in at the emergency entrance of the hospital. "What are we doing here?" The hospital was one of my least favorite places to visit.

"I may have broken the suspect's arm." Officer After looked sideways at me. "By accident." I followed at a safe distance as Officer After dragged Demetrius out of the car and led him into the emergency room.

Tiffany met me in the entrance with a violent hug that nearly knocked me down. "It was so exciting to listen on the scanner to what was going on! I wish we could trade places!"

"Be careful what you wish for," I said as Officer After came back alone. "Tiffany, this is Officer After, who arrested you. Officer After, this is Tiffany Hart, who doesn't remember you."

They shook hands more cordially than they should have. Officer After didn't have a problem with *her* touching him while he was in uniform.

"I am so sorry," Tiffany giggled and gushed. "You know how it is when you're drunk."

"No, he doesn't," I said. "He's been sober since birth."

"Me too!" Tiffany said. "Until last Saturday." She tilted her head annoyingly. Officer After showed his dimples.

"But I *do* remember him," she said. "You know who this is, don't you, Meg?"

Officer After's dimples faded.

"Mr. Harrison, my yearbook faculty sponsor, also taught AP English last year. John was the only John in that class." She touched Officer After lightly on the hand. He didn't flinch. She prattled on, "But his full name had such a ring to it that Mr. Harrison used the whole thing, *Johnafter*. The seniors told the yearbook staff about it, and we all called him Johnafter, too. It was a running joke that if we couldn't decide which picture to use in a certain place, we'd say, 'It's the perfect place for Johnafter.'"

"So he's in the yearbook fifty times?" I asked.

"We didn't have any pictures of him. No social shots. We decided he must be very antisocial." She elbowed him in the ribs. "No, just his senior portrait and his track team picture. He was on the track team that won the state championship last year, with Will Billingsley and Rashad Lowry and Skip Clark. And he dated Angie Pettit. *And*"—she pointed at him as more came back to her—"he was in Spanish class with you and me, Meg."

I turned to him. "*¡De verdad!*"

"*Sí.*" He eyed me warily.

"I missed that completely," I said. "I must have been in the back of the class, smoking meth and hacking the Department of Defense computers. So, Johnafter, you're only eighteen years old?"

6

I'm *nineteen*," he said self-righteously, as if this made all the difference in the world.

Then he cut off my outraged protest by informing me that even though his shift was over, he would have to stay late (or *early*, since it was 6 A.M.) to wait for the Suspect to Receive Medical Attention and Transport him back to the Detention Facility in his Vehicle. Tiffany offered to drive me back to the police station so I could get my motorcycle. Officer After slipped into the emergency room to guard Demetrius.

One night down, four to go.

Before my shift at the diner started, I ran inside the trailer to snatch last year's yearbook. Throughout the morning, between cooking orders of bacon and eggs, I flipped through the pages.

Alphabetically, he appeared on the first page of senior photos, where *After, John* should have been. But his name was printed *Johnafter* instead. That Mr. Harrison was a real card.

I double-checked the name, because the photo wasn't the cop. It was a senior in the fake tux they made boys wear, with a thin face and longish blond hair. Like a normal boy.

The only thing I recognized was the heavy-lidded dark eyes. At first. But as I studied him, the sensitive mouth seemed familiar. And the chin. Last night in the dark car, the only thing I could see clearly most of the time was his chin in the glow from the radio.

In fact, the longer I stared at this normal boy, the clearer the memory became of glancing at him in Spanish class last year. We passed yesterday's graded homework down the rows and leafed through the pile to pull our own sheets out. One page was always decorated with intricate doodles in the margins, careful little illustrations of the Spanish words. *Perro. Sombrero. Corazón.* I watched where this paper went. To an older boy with blond hair in his eyes, cute but shy, not my type. Not the type to like girls with purple hair, or whatever color mine was that month. Anyway, he wouldn't look at me, or if he did, not for long. I would have remembered his dark eyes.

I stared into those eyes in the yearbook photo. I examined the caption underneath. *Johnafter. Track 1, 2, 3, 4. Track Team Captain 4. ACT High Scorer 4.* He got the highest score in the school on the ACT. So did Tiffany.

I was called upon to spoon up some cheese grits just then, but I puzzled over the problem in my head. Something didn't fit with Johnafter.

Just a few years ago, our town was in the middle of nowhere. Lately Birmingham had spread out to meet us. The outskirts of the metropolitan area were only a few miles away. Our small town had lost some of its charm and retained all its backwardness. Families moved to this area from up north to work in the car factories springing up everywhere. Not knowing any better, they bought the cheap houses being built here. They stayed here until they figured out it was no fun and moved closer to Birmingham. So for all practical purposes, our town was still in the middle of nowhere, but now we had a Target.

If you were college material, right after graduating from our high school you escaped to UAB. Then you found a professional job and settled in Birmingham, never to return. Except on special occasions, such as passing through on your way to the beach.

If you weren't college material, you settled here in town. You had a baby at nineteen and *then* thought, duh, it's too bad I don't have an education, because I need a job. After a few years of working as a janitor, then a telemarketer, then a vinyl-siding salesman, you opened a shitty little diner. Your ingrate daughter got sick and dyed her hair blue. What a disappointment. You wanted said ingrate daughter to remain in town and keep your restaurant out of trouble by doing a large portion of the work for free. But alas, your daughter was college material. If she could keep out of jail.

What you did not do was make the highest score in the school on the ACT, then decide to cut your blond hair off, put on twenty pounds of muscle, become a cop, and stay here.

Something had happened to Johnafter.

I peered across the bag of chopped onions at the yearbook on the counter. I stared at his photo, with my hands over my mouth. And I realized that something was happening to *me*. For the first time in my life, I had a crush. On a cop. Who was never leaving this town.

Beware the Ides of March.

WHEN I GOT OFF WORK AT two in the afternoon, I rode my motorcycle to the city park. I could have jogged my daily five miles up and down the highway in front of Eggstra! Eggstra!, but I preferred the park. The hospital and rehab center were nearby. Lots of people with knee injuries or multiple sclerosis gimped along the track. It made you think that if they could do it, you could do it. Even if you had just spent eight hours flipping pancakes at Eggstra! Eggstra! on top of eight hours being faked out by a teenage cop.

As always, I stretched my muscles in front of the decorative park gate tiled with red, blue, and yellow handprints from my elementary school. Tiffany's handprint was there, and Brian's, and even Eric's. Mine was toward the bottom-left corner. I still remembered how thrilled I was to see my handprint and name on the wall for the first time, back when I was young and dorky(er). I thought I was famous. Along with everybody else in the third and fourth grades. Now I regretted that a little piece of me would be cemented to this place forever.

I braced myself on the wall with one hand, put my leg behind me, and pulled on my ankle to stretch my quadriceps. My head throbbed and my blood tingled from too much caffeine.

The trees in the park held tight to the tiniest bright green leaves. The sky was so blue it looked fake, and the yellow daffodils looked plastic, like in a cemetery. This told me I was *really* sleepy and/or I *really* needed to get out of town.

And jogging toward me came the ghost of Johnafter.

I think I actually did a double take. His shirt was off, showing the sort of six-pack abs I saw all the time on TV but rarely in person. His white skin glowed against the bright greens and yellows of the park. Probably from living in the dark on night shift. His blond hair looked white, too, and from this distance, his dark eyes were holes in his face.

He didn't look like a forty-year-old cop to me anymore. I didn't see how I had ever made this mistake, either. And he didn't look like the boy from the yearbook. He looked like what he was, a nineteen-year-old with a fantastic body. Get this—I resisted the urge to hide behind the tile wall. *I* felt *shy* in front of him. Like I admired him from afar, but I knew I didn't have a chance with him. Suddenly I wished my hair was not blue.

He jogged to a stop in front of me and panted a few times to get his breath back. Finally he said, "Hey," as if I was some girl from school instead of his prisoner.

"Hey," I said.

He looked at the wall. "Are you on here?"

I put my leg down and kicked my handprint on the wall to show him. I picked up my other ankle behind me.

He bent down to look at my handprint. "Mmph," he said. "Near Eric."

This irked me for some reason. "Are *you* on here?" I asked quickly. As I said it, I realized I'd been scanning the wall for his name the entire time I'd been stretching.

He walked to the opposite end of the wall and reached way up to put his hand over a handprint. It was almost as far from mine as possible.

I craned my neck to see. "Why is yours the only one on the wall that's black?"

"I went through a Goth phase when I was nine." He looked pointedly at me. "I grew out of it."

Did he mean my blue hair was immature? Ass. I said, "And you grew into your cop phase."

He turned without a word, walked into the parking lot a few paces away, and opened the door of a pickup truck. Great, I'd pissed him off. Riding around with him tonight would be fun fun fun.

To cover his naked muscles, he pulled on an Audioslave T-shirt I remembered him wearing in Spanish class last year. Only it fit him more tightly now. He lit a cigarette, slammed the truck door, and sauntered back to me.

I gestured to the cigarette. "What do you think you're doing? Flaunting your youth and good health in front of the cripples?"

His brown eyes widened at me, and he glanced toward an old lady moving at glacier pace on her walker. "It's the one thing I do wrong." He took a drag and sighed through his nose like he did when he was frustrated, but this time he exhaled smoke. "It keeps me awake. I'm tired. I'm always tired. The human body is not designed to work from ten P.M. to six A.M."

"Have you tried coffee? Mountain Dew? Red Bull?"

"That would keep me up too long. I want to sleep when I get home. I already tried and failed for eight hours. After my days off, my first day back is always the hardest. I came here to run and tire myself out." The picture of health took another drag from his cigarette. "Did you just get up?"

"No, I just got off work."

"Work!" He ran one hand back through his hair with a puzzled expression, as if he couldn't quite believe it was gone. "Where?"

"Eggstra! Eggstra!"

"For how long?"

"Since your shift was over."

"God. Why?"

"My parents are at Graceland. I was supposed to go to Miami on the senior trip." If he'd been in uniform, I probably would have added some sharp pricklies to this, such as, "I can't go to the beach thanks to you, bastard." Strange how I could say this to an enormous cop, but not to a cute blond boy in an Audioslave T-shirt. "They thought it was safe to leave town when I was leaving, too. Now that I'm staying, they need something else to keep me nailed down. Like Purcell, the asshole cook from last night, calling them to say I haven't shown up for my shift or something. They don't trust me. I wonder why not."

He didn't take the bait. He just shook his head and *sympathized*, of all things. "That's a brutal schedule. Why aren't you in bed now?"

"I have to run every day."

"To lose weight? Please say no."

"What's that supposed to mean?"

"It means . . ." He pulled at the hair on the back of his head. "Girls always think they need to lose weight, and you don't need to lose weight."

I stood up straight and covered my tummy with my hands. "You're saying I'm too skinny."

He took a long, thoughtful drag and exhaled as he spoke. "No. You're not."

Was he saying I was fat in all the right places? I put my hands on my hips, pushed my shoulders forward a little for enhancement of cleavage in my V-neck T-shirt, and leaned to the left to stretch my side. I guess I probably looked pretty good, if you were into blue hair and extreme fatigue.

But he was a frightened horse about to bolt. He wore that expression he tended to wear when I got too close to him, the oh-my-God-she's-trying-to-seduce-me-and-I-don't-like-it look.

I gave up and relaxed my shoulders. "You're talking about Angie Pettit. She doesn't count. She's a midget. She's so cute and petite you want to pinch her head off."

Johnafter took one last short drag from the cigarette, threw it down, and squashed it into the dirt with the heel of his running shoe. He imagined the cigarette butt was my head.

"I take it you're still dating her," I said.

"No. She broke up with me last fall."

Ah, the cigarette was *Angie's* head. "Why'd she break up with you?"

Now he put both hands in what was left of his hair and slowly stroked backward. Either this was a show of discomfort he controlled carefully when he was in uniform, or he wanted me to notice his huge triceps. Believe me, I noticed.

"Because I'm a cop," he said, "and I live in this town, and she didn't want to get stuck here. She wanted to go to UAB."

This surprised me. Angie did not seem like college material. She seemed like cosmetology school material. Not that this was an insult. I knew from experience it was very difficult to get hair to take blue color and hold it for any length of time.

Oh, why not. I leaned to the right and asked him, "Are you dating anyone now?"

"What?" He stepped out of the way to let a jogger pass on the track. Watching the retreat of the woman's large pink terry-cloth buttocks, he explained, "There's not a lot of opportunity for me to date, or even meet someone. I'm not awake when other people are awake."

"What do you do for fun?"

"Fun," he mused. "What's your definition of *fun?*"

"It's not a good sign if you have to think about it that hard. Basically, your life sucks because of this job. Why do you want this job?"

"It's something I've wanted to do since I was a kid."

I wanted to scream, *Why?* But I knew I'd get another non-answer. "So, you ran track, right?"

"In high school?"

I straightened up. "You just graduated nine months ago. You really do act like you're forty years old."

He blinked. "I do?"

"*Yes*, in high school. Tiffany said you were friends with Will Billingsley and Rashad Lowry and those track guys."

"Yeah," he said slowly.

"Do y'all still hang out?"

"No, they're at UAB."

"Why didn't *you* go to UAB?"

"I told you," he said. "I wanted to be a cop." He looked around the park like this conversation was making him uncomfortable and he needed a way out.

"Why didn't you get a degree first in, whatsit, cop studies?"

"Criminal justice," he said. "I wanted to be a cop sooner."

"Won't you need that degree eventually to move up in the department?"

"Yes. I don't necessarily want to move up. I'm happy doing this."

Yeah, you look happy, I wanted to say. But this convo was interesting. I couldn't sound too rude and give him the excuse he needed to walk away. "If Tiffany hadn't spilled the beans, were you going to tell me who you are?"

"You mean that I'm nineteen and we went to high school together?"

Duh, I thought. I couldn't say *Duh*. Too obvious. My brain would not cough up an alternative witticism. I hadn't slept in thirty hours.

"I wasn't trying to hide it from you," he said. "But I'm in a position of authority, and I'm trying to control people in sometimes dangerous situations. Naturally I'm not going to offer to people, 'By the way, here's where I'm vulnerable.'"

"Vulnerable," I repeated thoughtfully. Yes, this had been a very interesting convo. I'd discovered all sorts of buttons I could push to make him feel vulnerable and keep him off my ass for the rest of the week.

And then he turned on me. "So, why *do* you run? Not for health. That doesn't seem like you."

Where was that low hum coming from? I looked around, probably rather frantically. It was a streetlight malfunctioning behind Johnafter, flickering on in the middle of the sunny day, splashing additional light on his white head and shoulders.

"More out of blind fear," I blurted before I thought.

He stepped forward and opened his mouth to ask me for more.

"See you tonight," I said, and dashed off.

I was relieved when I finished my first lap and saw that his truck was gone. I felt a lot more comfortable with him in his police uniform. Impudence in the face of authority—*that* I could do. And after running the obstacle course of emotions in the park with hunky Johnafter, I much preferred a good old-fashioned high-speed car chase.

7

"Hold on," he said.

This suggestion was completely unnecessary. I'd fastened my seat belt tonight. Still, I clung to the door and the dashboard for dear life as he slung the cop car around 180 degrees.

He sped the car in the opposite direction after the suspect. The engine hummed low, then higher as he floored it. "Siren would be nice," he said.

"Oh, sorry." I flicked a switch on the box below the dashboard and got the chirping sound. "Sorry, sorry." I flicked another switch to produce the proper wail.

Lois had fed us a call that drug deals were going down on the wrong side of town. In typical Johnafter fashion, we snuck around the streets with the headlights off until we surprised the driver of this Kia in mid-buy. Officer Leroy and some other cops had stayed behind to clean up the sellers while John and I chased the buyer who got away.

"Where do you think you're going?" John murmured. John talked to himself a lot—I'd noticed this last night. Actually he was talking to suspects who couldn't hear him. My guess was that he'd been on night shift by himself way too long. "Please, not downtown."

"Yes, downtown," I said, as if he were talking to me. We flew through the deserted streets and went airborne over the speed bump beside the jail/courthouse/city hall. "Yee-haw!" I hollered. "I've always wanted to do that."

"Try not to make us sound like *The Dukes of Hazzard*," he said. "At least not with the window open."

"Sorry, sorry."

"Not the roundabout," he said. Sure enough, the Kia entered the traffic circle in the center of town. We chased him around it twice.

"Okay, damn it," John said, and I knew what he was about to do. At the last second, he jerked the car off the roundabout, down a street that was hard to see if you didn't know it was there. He accelerated through three turns and re-entered the roundabout to cut the Kia off.

The Kia was too wise. He was out of the roundabout already. His taillights glowed way down at the high school. John cussed.

"You need some backup here, John."

He nodded toward the CB. "That's what Lois is telling me. There's no one to help me. They took the sellers into custody, and now they've all gone to a wreck at the Birmingham Junction."

"What if he starts shooting at us?"

"You watch too much TV. He's small-time, like Eric." John whipped out of the roundabout and floored it again. "I really don't want to let this guy go. There's no way my Ford is outrun by a Kia. That's just wrong."

"John," I said. Below the siren, below the motor, a low hum vibrated the car.

He sped toward the railroad crossing, where red lights flashed in warning.

"John!" I gasped at the same instant he stomped the brakes. We skidded to a stop in front of the blinking signals. The Kia kept going, squeaking past the locomotive with inches to spare.

John and I watched the progression of train cars. We'd lost him.

Sighing through his nose, John reached to the CB to call Lois. There it was again. I'd thought I smelled cologne several times in the hour since John's shift started tonight. Not an overpowering slather—just a little, so I caught only a whiff of it when he moved.

It couldn't be him. He wouldn't dare make himself smell sexy to the blue-haired prisoner he found so distasteful. But I was pretty sure nothing else in this 1990s Crown Victoria smelled that good. I leaned closer, pretending to examine the siren controls, and tried to sniff him without letting out a big snort.

Unsuccessfully. He said, "I have some Kleenex in the trunk."

Better to admit what I was doing than let him think I had postnasal drip. "You smell good."

He stared at me, and my heart turned over. After last night riding around with my window rolled down in the cold, he'd wised up. He wore his leather cop jacket, which made him look that much more sharp and dangerous. His dark eyes pierced me, but the glow from the downtown streetlights softened his strong jaw and those sensitive lips. And his whole body was bathed in red as the warning lights from the railroad crossing blinked on, off, on, off, on.

Off, for good. The train was gone.

He looked ahead, into the empty street. "Where would you go?" he asked the suspect. Then he turned back to me. "Help me search for the Kia in parking lots as we pass. Sometimes they're that stupid."

Oh sure. I would search parking lots on the way to our destination. I knew exactly where we were going.

Sure enough, a few miles later he turned off the main road and onto the dirt road to the bridge.

"We're driving down here *again?*" I exclaimed. We'd already visited the bridge at the beginning of the shift.

He unhooked the CB from the dashboard and handed it to me without taking his eyes off the road. "If you ever feel threatened, press this button to call Lois. She'll send another car to save you from me." He sounded almost hurt.

"I don't feel *threatened*. It's just that a criminal isn't going to hide where there's only one way out and you're blocking it. Criminals don't trap themselves."

He continued down the road anyway, and I thought harder about what he'd said. *Threatened?* Yes, the thought of him taking advantage of me had flashed across my mind when he first arrested me at the bridge, and last night. But that was before I knew him. It hadn't crossed my mind tonight.

It had crossed *his*.

And he was wearing cologne.

"How did I end up with you?" I asked.

He turned to me, wide-eyed. "What?" The car lunged over a rock, and he put his eyes back on the road.

"Why am I riding in your police car instead of the ambulance or the fire truck? Did y'all draw straws, and you were the lucky winner? I'll bet everyone was hoping for Tiffany, but alas."

I half expected him to look all shiny and new at the mention of Tiffany. Or to protest too much, giving himself away.

He didn't answer.

"John?"

"I picked you," he said quietly.

I swallowed. It probably didn't mean anything. At least, not what I wanted it to.

"Why'd you pick me? So you could get me alone on Hot Date 911? I'm telling Angie."

"No, I'm not coming on to you at *all*," he said, voice rising. "I don't want you to get the wrong idea. No."

"Right!" I snapped. I didn't want to snap. I never really thought he liked me for real. It was just that he made the idea sound *loathsome*. "How could I suggest something so ridiculous?

You wouldn't be attracted to a loudmouthed blue-haired girl. Of course, Eric is. Of course, Eric is charged with multiple felonies."

"I'm not sure I'd call that an attraction," he said. "From the way you talk about him, he's not much of a boyfriend. He's more of a john."

I counted to ten silently. I had enough self-control to keep from punching the police. By eight, I could hear the jealousy in his voice.

He was jealous.

That was no excuse. I swiped my notebook out of the floorboard and wrote *he's not much of a boyfriend—he's more of a John.*

"Meg."

"You called me a prostitute."

"I realize now I shouldn't have put it—"

"Thanks, Officer After."

"It's just because your relationship with him seems to be nothing but sex—"

"So why can't—"

"—if you think he wouldn't even save you from an oncoming train."

"So why can't *I* be the john?" I asked.

"You can be the john."

"Why can't *he* be the prostitute, and *I* can be the john?"

"You can be the john. God!" He stopped the car in the clearing with a jerk. The headlights shone across the gravel but didn't quite touch the end of the bridge.

He turned to me with his arms crossed on his chest. Which of course he should not have done, because I knew exactly what *that* meant. He felt vulnerable.

"Look," he said, "I didn't mean to get into all this. Let's not even joke about the idea that I picked a suspect to hook up with. I mean, here we are, driving around all night alone in the dark, and I have a gun and handcuffs."

What he was trying to get across is how threatening this situation should have been for me. But I didn't see it that way. I got chills in the darkness at the thought of him coming on to me. Granted, I was allergic to handcuffs, and I didn't want to be threatened with a gun. But the whole scenario smacked of some X-rated leather-heavy adult movie, and suddenly I very much wanted to be an adult. With Johnafter.

I couldn't see his eyes clearly in the darkness, only the lower half of his face. He bit his bottom lip gently. Vulnerable.

"Why *did* you pick me?" I asked.

"You remind me of someone."

"With blue hair?" I laughed. "Who?"

"No. You know that story you asked me about the first night? Those kids getting killed on the bridge?"

I nodded at the freight train I knew was about to hit me.

"Kids think it's a ghost story," he said, "but adults still remember it as a tragedy."

"How do *you* remember it?"

"Both ways." He sighed through his nose, this time a long, slow sigh. "You remind me of that girl who died. She was a lot older than me, but she lived in my neighborhood. You have the same eyes."

I blinked. My eyes were blue. Probably they were accentuated by my blue hair. I hadn't checked. I knew green hair hadn't done much for them.

I felt a low rumble in the floorboard of the car, stronger than the car's engine. Automatically now, I turned to the tracks and saw the white circle of headlight. The train had traveled through town and reached the bridge.

John continued. "Both of you have the same idea that you need some bad boy to show you life. You know he'll get you in trouble, and you don't care. You'd follow him anywhere." He shouted above the train's horn, which was excruciatingly loud through my open window. "And the worst part is, you won't admit that to yourself. A boy will be your downfall."

"Oh." I tried the door handle. "Let me out." I slapped the door with the flat of my hand. "Let me out, John, I swear to God!" I started to climb through the window at the same time I tried the handle again. The door swung open over the gravel, and I fell on my ass on the sharp rocks.

I thought I heard John call to me over the noise filling the clearing, but I just ran, away from him, toward the train.

The captain of the state championship high school track team caught me by the arm in two seconds. "Meg, come on. We're supposed to be looking for that Kia. We don't have time for this."

I pulled my arm away. "We don't have time for me to be

completely creeped out that I'm riding around with you because I remind you of a dead girl. But we have time to drive down a dirt road and make sure the bridge is still here." I whirled around and gestured into the dark where I assumed the bridge was. "Well, I'll be damned. It's still here. It hasn't lifted up its girders and waded downstream."

"Meg—"

"You don't know me. You don't know anything about me. You see me once, trespassing, stoned, which I might add is somewhat out of character for me no matter what you choose to think, and you decide you have me all figured out? Graduating from the police academy does not qualify you as a psychiatrist."

"Was it your idea to go up on that bridge?"

"No."

"It wasn't that other girl's idea, either."

The train passed, but this time I didn't turn to watch its taillights disappear into the trees. I was locked in a stubborn stare with Johnafter's dark eyes.

The racket of wheels clacking on the rails lifted, leaving only the low hum of the police car underneath. This deep in the forest, tree frogs should have been screaming in the trees, but it was only March. They hadn't woken up yet.

"If I could—" he started, then realized how loud his voice sounded. He cleared his throat and said quietly, "If I could save just one person, just you, all this would be worth it."

"All *what* would be worth it? Carting me around for a week? Or being a cop in the first place?"

There was more gentle lip-biting. He crossed his arms and looked toward the railroad tracks. He wanted to melt into the shadows, I knew, but too bad. He was standing in the beam of the police car headlights, as brightly lit as if he were number one in a police lineup.

"John, did you become a cop just so you can save people from the bridge?"

"It's not that simple," he told the tracks.

"That's screwed up, John."

He turned back to me. "It's not that simple," he said again, through his teeth.

This was really a problem for him. I took in the whole picture of him, dark eyes, scowl, crossed arms.

Then I thought about what *I* must look like in the headlights' beam. I had crossed my arms at some point without knowing it. I looked the same as John, but with the blue eyes of a dead girl.

We stood there by the bridge, at this impasse, for what seemed like a long time.

Finally I took a deep breath and uncrossed my arms with effort, letting them hang by my sides. I felt naked. "The Kia knows you're looking for him and you're probably working all night. He plans to hide out somewhere until morning, then blend into the rush hour traffic headed to Birmingham. In the meantime, he knows you're the only one chasing him. He figures he's not that important. So he'll pick a hiding place that has two ways out, like I said."

John uncrossed his arms. "For instance?"

"The quarry. The airport. Behind the rental storage buildings."

He nodded at the car. "Let's go."

On the bumpy drive back to the main road, I tried to gauge whether we were on speaking terms again, or whether we were going to spend the rest of the night plus three more in this uncomfortable silence. I tried it out. "Why are you bothering? He dumped the shit out the window fifteen minutes ago."

"Even if I caught him with something, it wouldn't stick. Usually doesn't. Or he'd be out in six months. I just like to scare them."

Right before he pulled onto the main road, he turned up the radio, probably so he wouldn't have to talk to me again. He still bit his lip gently. But by the time we reached the dirt road through the woods that eventually would snake behind the storage buildings, he'd recovered. With a glance at me, he said, "You know an awful lot about hiding from cops."

"I don't make daily drug buys, if that's what you're thinking. I go parking."

He grinned, showing his dimples.

"Don't act like you're above it," I laughed. "Next weekend, I'd better not find you in all my parking places."

"I don't need to go parking anymore. I have an apartment."

"That's right. I forget you're the big nineteen." I had assumed he still lived with his parents. Now I wondered what it would be like to make out (or more) in a boy's apartment. No cops to sneak up on you. No parents to walk in on you.

With Johnafter.

Who liked me only because I reminded him of a dead girl. So, never mind.

He cut the headlights, and the car crept to the edge of a cliff. Below us, we could see the roof of the Kia behind the storage buildings.

"If you drive down there," I said, "he'll just escape the other way. That's what he's counting on. You have to walk down there, point your gun at him, and yell at him in that charming way you have."

John radioed to Lois and opened the door. As he got out, he tossed at me, "You have a brilliant criminal mind."

"Thanks, I think." I watched him walk down the road through the forest with his hand on his gun. The floodlights over the storage buildings hummed low.

8

"We're doing Mickey D's instead of the diner tonight?" I asked as he steered the car into the McDonald's parking lot.

"No, too early."

True. 11:30 P.M. was way too early for lunch.

"I just need to chase off these loiterers," he said.

The curly-haired loiterer I recognized as Will Billingsley, John's alleged former friend from the track team. I didn't know him that well, but I knew who he was. Everybody knew who Will was. Will was very friendly. The redhead was Skip Clark, and the hunky black guy might even have been Rashad Lowry.

John must feel cocky after successfully apprehending the small-time drug buyer. He'd impounded the Kia. Now he was going after his friends? Yes, they were standing where teenage loiterers stood to see and be seen, at the edge of the playground, by the picnic tables. But they also were eating french fries, so they were patrons. They couldn't technically be considered loiterers.

John waited for me to round the car, then crossed the parking lot with me. I was about to suggest he reconsider his tactics with the town's youth when Will called, "Little Johnny Afterrrrrrrr!"

John broke into a huge smile, dimples and all.

As John reached their circle, Rashad leaned in to give him a bear hug, but Will held Rashad back. "Don't touch him while he's in uniform," Will said.

"Apologies," Rashad said. "I forgot I am not to touch the incredible expanding Johnafter."

The fit track team boys towered over me, and John was only a little taller than them. But they gave him more room than they gave one another. The dark blue uniform and broad chest and I'm-in-charge stance created a bubble around him. He was one of them, but not. One of these things was not like the others.

"Vat have you been up to, Governor?" Skip asked with an Arnold Schwarzenegger accent.

"The relentless pursuit of crime," John said. He pronounced *crime* with a long southern drawl and a wink. Then he burst into laughter with the rest of them.

Seeing him jogging at the park had cracked the window so I could peek into his soul. Seeing him with his friends threw the window wide open.

He was *so* nineteen.

As if he could read my mind, he turned to me and whispered, "You didn't see me laughing." To the others he said, "Don't make me laugh while I'm in uniform."

Skip asked John something else about work, and Will turned to me. "I know you from high school. Meg, right?"

"That's right."

"Why are you riding around with John? I'll bet you're one of those suspects from the bridge."

John called across the circle, "No, she's undercover."

"Oh, like Sydney on *Alias*," Will said. Of the possible comparisons, that was pretty flattering. He tugged a lock of my hair to see if it was a wig.

Disapproval flashed across John's face. I wondered whether no one was supposed to touch *me* while he was in uniform, either.

Will noticed John's look. He moved his hand away. Loudly enough for John to hear, he asked me, "What do you think of Officer After so far?"

"He's an excellent driver."

"He wasn't always," Will said. "I taught him to drive. The *police academy* may have helped some." He pronounced *police academy* strangely, the same way John did. This was an old, old joke between them.

"We're headed to the Redneck Riviera tomorrow," Rashad said to John. "You want to come?" That must have been why they were hanging out around this town. They'd stopped here to visit their parents on their way to the Florida Panhandle for spring break.

"I already asked him," Will said. "He has to work."

"Just because you're not in school doesn't mean you don't deserve a spring break," Rashad told John. "Even the fuzz needs love."

"Looks like he's already got some," Skip said.

Everybody looked at Skip blankly.

Did he mean me?

"Anyway," John said, "I don't think I'd be welcome, if Eric's going."

"He's not going," Skip said. "His parents grounded him because of the bridge incident. Can you imagine? Grounded."

Indeed I couldn't imagine. John and Eric were the same age. John was a policeman, and Eric was grounded.

"He's not too grounded," Rashad said. "I saw his Beamer five minutes ago."

"Not grounded from driving his Beamer," Will said. "Just grounded from driving two hundred and fifty miles to the beach. Come on. You don't expect *grounded* to mean the same thing for him as it does for everyone else, do you?"

Skip took a hit off an imaginary roach. "I am better than you," he said in a stoned voice. "I am a high. School. Graduate!"

Rashad guffawed, but John and Will didn't laugh. In fact, Will seemed to be giving Rashad and Skip a warning look they didn't see.

John pointed at me. "Coffee?" I nodded, and he turned and walked toward McDonald's. I stopped myself from calling after him how I took it: cream and three sugars. After one night with me, John knew how I took my coffee. We drank a lot of coffee.

Will watched John until the door to McDonald's closed behind him. Then he yelled, "Skip, you dummy. What did you say that for?"

"What?" Skip asked innocently.

"Making fun of John for being a high. School. Graduate?"

"I was making fun of Eric, not John."

"Besides," Rashad said, "John's more than a high. School. Graduate. He's a graduate of the *police academy*." He pronounced it strangely, too. They were all in on the joke. They must have really ribbed John about it last summer when they finished high school and everyone but John left town.

Will shook his head and turned to me. "So, you're dating Eric? What's *that* about?"

"Not really dating," I said.

"I thought you were dating. I thought John said he caught you on the bridge together."

"More like consorting."

Will gasped and put his hand to his mouth in mock horror. Luckily, Rashad and Skip were talking to each other and didn't notice. Otherwise, I might have kneed Will.

"In case you haven't figured this out," he said, "Eric is bad news. You should stay away from him."

I shrugged. "Eric's not that evil. It's a rite of passage to get in trouble when you're a freshman in college, isn't it? Finding yourself or whatever."

"Eric found himself a long time ago," Skip called. "He found himself to be a stoner."

"Maybe you didn't know him that well in school," Will told me, "but we all learned our lesson about Eric in sixth grade, when he huffed gasoline on a Boy Scout camping trip."

"And John told the Scoutmaster," Rashad offered.

"And John told the Scoutmaster!" Will said, grinning. "It's a blood feud by now."

I shrugged again. "Like I said, I'm not serious with Eric, anyway."

"How about . . ." Will nodded toward McDonald's.

"You mean am I serious with *John?*" My heart raced at this idea—exciting and terrifying at the same time. I reminded myself that being serious with John wasn't a possibility, just a misunderstanding on Will's part. "John doesn't like me very much."

All three of them made *nuh-uh* noises.

"When y'all walked over here from the car," Will said, "he had his hand on your—" He put his hand at waist level behind me, without touching me.

"He had his hand on my ass?"

"No," they said.

"Behind your back," Rashad said. "Like you're dating or something." He put his hand behind Skip's back. Skip hit him.

"It was enough for all three of us to notice," Will said.

I wanted to say, *But my hair is blue!* I decided this went without saying.

"And he smells good," Will said.

Skip took a big whiff of Rashad. "You smell like Teen Spirit."

While Skip and Rashad shoved each other, I looked up at Will and said quietly, "I remind him of the girl who got killed on the bridge."

Will went very still. "Oh. Right. You messed with his bridge. He's been obsessed with the bridge since he was nine. What he lacks in clarity, he makes up for in consistency."

"Here comes the heat," Skip said. "Act natural."

John came back to the circle, handed me one of the cups of coffee, then stepped between Will and me. Will moved over. John looked around at our faces. "'Fess up."

"Nevah," Skip said in the Schwarzenegger voice.

"I ran into Angie in Target," Will told John. "She's staying with her folks in town this week."

"Why doesn't *she* go to Florida?" John asked.

"She says she hopes she'll see you while she's here."

John gaped. "Why? *She* broke up with *me*!"

"Girls are icky and have cooties." Will nodded to me. "Pardon."

"Angie's coming to my party when we get back Saturday night," Rashad said. "You can make it to that at least, John. Whether you want to see her or not."

"I have to work," John said.

"There is much work to be done for da people of California," said Skip Schwarzenegger.

"Would you like to come to my party?" Rashad asked me. "Eric will probably be there. I've never known Eric to miss a party, even when he wasn't invited."

John said, "No," just as I asked, "Where is it?"

"Around the corner from Five Points," Rashad said. "You know where that is?"

I loved Five Points, the artsy section of Birmingham near UAB, filled with cool shops and apartment buildings from the 1920s. In the center of the intersection was a fountain with statues of animals. A big ram held a book and read to a bear, a rabbit stacked on a turtle, and other forest creatures. Some people said the ram was the Devil. He had horns and hooves and told stories to other beasties. And five frogs in the shape of a pentagram spat water at him. But the fountain sat in front of a beautiful old church, with a glass-tiled synagogue down the street. You would think the Devil would be canceled out by the houses o' worship.

"I'll be there," I said at the same time John said, "No. She's seventeen." While Rashad gave me the apartment building and number, John edged closer behind me. "Rashad, she's seventeen."

I looked around at John. "I'll be eighteen in May."

"The party is in March." The small radio on his shoulder suddenly buzzed with static and Lois's voice. He spoke a few words into it, then put his hand on the back of my neck. "Official police business."

"Leave da woman," Skip said. "She must pass da state inspection."

John's hand tightened briefly on my neck, then let go. He was behind me, so I couldn't see the look he gave Skip. It must have been ugly. Skip put up both his hands. "I'm kidding!"

John and I headed back to the car. When we got in, John

started the engine, and I punched the correct siren. It should have been exciting to go investigate another crime.

But all I could think about was John's hand on the back of my neck. It had happened so fast—there, and then gone. The hair on my scalp stood on end anyway.

As John drove out of the parking lot, Rashad and Skip talked together, and Will watched our car. Rashad poked Will's shoulder, but Will continued to watch us. He never took his eyes off us. As if he expected the cop car to burst into flames.

WE SPED ACROSS TOWN, SIREN SHRIEKING. But by the time we got to the crime scene, the burglary was over. Neighbors said the victims were out of town for spring break. Officer Leroy was standing guard.

There wasn't much for John to do. Just a little Official Police Business such as securing the scene and smoking a cigarette and waiting an hour for the detective to show up.

There was also a lot of Sullen Malarkey on John's part. I followed him around the ransacked house, stepping over broken furniture, trying to make conversation. Every time I asked him a question, he said, "Don't touch that."

"Do you work your way up from cop to detective eventually?"

"If you want to. I don't want to. Don't touch that."

"I see. You're all man, right? You don't want a desk job. You want the thrill of the hunt, the adrenaline rush."

"No. I just don't want to be a detective. They figure out what happened after the fact, when it's too late. I want to prevent it from happening. Don't touch that."

"Yeah, you were a lot of use to these folks. When they get back from vacation and see the Yankees stole their silver, they'll want to meet you and thank you in person. They might even buy you a Moon Pie."

"Meg, for the last time, you're tampering with evidence. Don't touch— Get out of here. Go wait for me in the Goddamn car."

I slammed the door of the crime scene on my way out.

Then I sat in the Goddamn car, lowered the windows, blasted the heat so I didn't freeze in the dark, and turned up the radio. "Dirty Little Secret" again. I'd figured out last night, after the sixth playing of "Dirty Little Secret," that no one bothered to man the radio station in the wee hours. They stacked twenty tunes in endless rotation. These songs were an odd mix, too, like someone had grabbed a handful of CDs and thrown them in the machine before they went home to bed.

My Chemical Romance, "The Ghost of You."

I put my feet up on the dashboard.

A sickly sweet Phil Collins song from a Disney movie.

The seat wouldn't recline. The metal grate that separated the front seat from the criminal seat was in the way. I lay my head against the door and closed my eyes.

Mariah Carey, "Touch My Body."

I leaned forward and turned up the volume as high as I

could stand it, just for spite. It was loud enough to wake the neighborhood, but I was tired enough to sleep through anything. I settled back and closed my eyes again.

"God damn it." John jerked open his door and turned the radio off, then sat down and cranked the engine. The detective's car was parked in front of us. I wondered if I'd gotten John in trouble. I didn't really care.

I took my feet off the dashboard.

A few minutes later, he pulled in at Eggstra! Eggstra! Excellent, we could share a meal in this mood. Good for the digestion.

I was further irked when he hung his leather cop jacket on the coatrack by the door, like he owned the place. I suppose that's what we had the coatrack there for. I'd just never seen anyone use it. Then he headed for the windmill table, like last night.

"Hold on, there, Officer," I said to his back. "I suffered through the windmill table when I thought you were forty years old. Now that I know you're nineteen, I'm putting my foot down."

He looked around the diner. "The what? Oh, you mean the windmill salt and pepper shakers."

"My mother collects salt and pepper shakers. My parents are easily amused." I gestured toward the corner. "I can't sit at the windmill table. It makes me claustrophobic. I always sit at the unicorn table by the window."

"I can't sit by the window. Too exposed."

He meant *too vulnerable*.

"Let's split the difference," he said. We sat down at the Elvis table. Purcell poured us both coffee, thank God.

"You really thought I was forty years old?" John asked. "What made you think that? My manly physique?"

His dark eyes challenged me. They were weapons that could hurt me. Here was the worst thing about them: I could tell that if Johnafter loved you, his dark eyes would be beautiful and friendly and warm. So every time he cut me down with a look that was cold and unfriendly and ugly, it was a double insult, a reminder of what I could never have. I found myself avoiding his dark eyes when I could.

"I think it's the hair," I said.

He touched the nape of his neck and just managed to stop himself from running his fingers through his growing-out military cut. "So." He slid one of the little Elvis busts toward him. Salt spilled out the King's nose. "You seem to get along really well with my friends."

That was the cause of the Sullen Malarkey? "For a full-time city employee, you sure are immature. When's your birthday?"

He spun Elvis so the salt flew in all directions. "December."

"You see? I'm one and a half years younger than you. Since boys are two years behind girls in maturity level, I'm really six months older than you."

He slid Elvis back in place, next to the sugar, and looked up at me. "That's for high school boys. I'm nineteen."

"Wow, *nineteen*. You probably haven't even finished growing yet."

He straightened in his seat and stretched his arms over his head. "So? I'm one of the tallest people on the force."

I almost laughed at the idea of our small-town police as a

Force. "I don't think you should be hired as a cop until you've reached your full adult height. It seems barbaric. I've never heard of a nineteen-year-old cop."

"You have to be twenty-one most places, but there are a few where you can be nineteen. Montgomery Police. Florida Highway Patrol."

"Seems like they'd have another cop riding with you. I mean, come on. You've only been *driving* for three years."

"They did. Leroy rode with me until last month. But they were in a hurry to get me in my own vehicle because it took someone else off graveyard shift." He yawned.

"Graveyard shift or not, it sounds like a huge compliment. If they put you on patrol by yourself, they trust you with their lives. Or at least their squad car."

"I guess. They also threatened me. They told me that I'd better not screw up, or . . . Have you seen *Braveheart?*"

"No."

"They cut off Mel Gibson's— Well. We're about to eat." He gave me a wan smile to go with the unhappy picture.

Even with a wan smile, his dimples showed.

"Now you look nineteen." I tried not to say it tenderly. "What'd you do between graduating from high school and starting this job? Party hearty?"

"No, I went to the *police academy.*"

"Right, the *police academy*. Please tell me you at least went out and got good and soused on your nineteenth birthday."

"No. I came in to work. It was my first day on the job. Night, I should say." He shifted to his authoritarian voice, calm on the surface with a threat underneath. "Most adults do not take any available opportunity to drink themselves into a stupor. You've been around Eric too long. Eric's not going to make it to thirty."

"Oh, good God. He's harmless."

"I wouldn't be too sure. Especially when he's around you. You never can tell with domestics. They're completely unpredictable."

"Domestic! We're not a domestic. We're not married. Ew." I squirmed at the thought. Which was probably what John wanted.

"That's what we call it," he said. "Domestic."

"That's what you call *what*? We're not living together. We're not serious at all."

"You're having sex."

Not for over a week, I thought to myself. But I was able to stop myself from saying it. I realized just in time how lame it would sound.

"Then you're a domestic," John said.

I didn't owe John an explanation. And I didn't think this crush I had on him would ever be anything but. Still, it bothered me that he considered me whore-like.

"The thing is," I said, "I really didn't want to with *him*. I wanted to in *general*."

This explanation probably did not reduce my whore-like profile.

"Anyway," I blathered on stupidly, "now I'm sort of sorry I did it, because he's nuts."

John nodded. "Domestic."

9

John held me with the dark look. Part of me wanted to embrace the dark look, chase it wherever it went, on the off chance I could convert it to my side. The rest of me wanted to dodge the dark look. I glanced around at the empty booths: butterfly table, cowboy boot table, Liberace table. I wished I could see the grill from here. I wondered how close our food was to being ready. Anything to distract him. And me.

"He's not your type," John said.

I looked back at John. "Of course he's my type. I won't make it to thirty, either."

He stared at me for a few seconds more, then blinked. "Not Eric. I meant Will."

"Will! Billingsley? Where are you getting this? McDonald's?"

He breathed deeply. Deeply enough that I thought he might

have been holding his breath while he waited for my response. His shoulders lowered, and he seemed to relax a little. "Okay, maybe there wasn't anything going on between you two at McDonald's—"

"He pulled my hair, John."

"—but I wanted to make sure you knew what a nice guy he is."

"And therefore not my type, huh?" God, how whore-like did John think I was? "I could try an experiment with a nice guy. I could teach him a thing or two."

His shoulders tensed again. "He's a nice guy, and he would fall in love with you, and you would break his heart."

I leaned forward until my boobs sat on the table like a set of oversize salt and pepper shakers. The tit table. "Just as well. I prefer boys to teach me rather than the other way around."

His dark look flicked to my boobs ever so briefly. Then his eyes met mine again. "It's spring break. School's out." He sipped his coffee like an adult.

I sipped my own coffee and studied him. The stubborn set to his jaw. The way he glanced toward the windows every few seconds to check for danger.

I knew what he was thinking. He wasn't really jealous, but it came out that way. We were a boy and a girl riding around at night together, and he didn't have any other distractions. He didn't want to date me. He was just interested in me, for lack of anything better to do. Because he was lonely. And because I'd given him a jump start the first night at the bridge by reminding him of the dead girl. There ought to be a Hallmark card for this.

"I would never date Will, even if he wasn't a nice guy," I said truthfully. "It was fun to flirt with him, but everyone knows he's like that with everybody. He makes people feel good about themselves. He's also one of those drama club types who says very funny things very loudly with large gestures, like he wants people to look at him."

John's brow knitted. "You're describing yourself."

"What?"

"That's why you don't like him."

"I'm not describing myself."

He smiled. "Don't tell me you don't want people to look at you. And you probably have lots of friends. You're charismatic."

"Charismatic," I acknowledged, "and kind of a bitch. I don't have any friends because I've pissed them all off. I stand people up."

His brow knitted again. "Why?"

"Oh . . . Boys ask me on dates, or girls ask me on girl outings. And it sounds like fun, and I want to go. But then, when it comes right down to it, I can't go through with it. I hate plans. I feel . . ." I searched for the word. "Handcuffed." I shuddered.

"Handcuffed to the plan?"

"To the other person."

"How do you date Eric, then?"

"We don't date."

"Right." John nodded. "You just screw."

Okay, that was too far. "John—"

He opened his hands on the table. "How are you ever going to have a relationship?"

"I guess I'll be alone."

I could almost see the wheels turning behind his dark eyes, processing this information, looking for a hole in the theory. "You've shown up in time for my shift both nights so far," he pointed out.

"Yeah, and it's taken a couple of years off my life."

"You planned to go to Miami for spring break."

I smiled sweetly at him. "Thanks for bringing *that* up. Yeah, I planned to go, which involved meeting the bus at a certain time. But I didn't plan to hang out with a certain person or do a certain thing once I got there. I was wide open."

He forgot and rubbed his hand on the short hair at the back of his head. Then he remembered and put his hand down. "You're friends with Tiffany."

And thanks for bringing *her* up. "Not really."

"Weren't you talking with her on the phone last night? In the vehicle?"

"She's the only person I knew who was awake then." This was inaccurate, since even Tiffany and the paramedics had been asleep when I called. "But I'll let you in on one plan I've already made. I'm going to Rashad's party Saturday night."

He bit his bottom lip.

"And while I'm there, maybe you could ride around on patrol with Tiffany. You seem to get along really well with *her*."

We both backed away from the table as Purcell reached between us with tattooed arms, setting down our plates. I hadn't realized how far forward we'd both been leaning.

"Tiffany is cute," John called from the other side of the booth, which seemed like yelling across the Grand Canyon in comparison with how we'd talked before. "She's nice. Not sexy, if that's what you're insinuating."

I wanted to inform Officer After that I was not insinuating a damn thing about Tiffany. I was fishing for information about myself alone.

And now I wondered if he was insinuating that I was *not* cute, that I was *not* nice. Which I had gathered. Or that I *was* sexy.

Oh hell, what was the matter with me? He wasn't even looking at me. He was wolfing down his lunch.

I picked up my fork. "Why don't you ask for the night off so *you* can go to the party?"

He glanced up from his food. "I can't ask off to go to a college party."

"Why not?"

"People ask off to go to their wife's high school reunion or their son's wedding. They don't ask off to go to a college party."

"They're not nineteen years old. Everyone should be able to ask off for what's important to them." I gestured to his plate. "Whatcha got there? Steak and eggs with steamed vegetables? Very healthy. Protein and vitamins, a runner's meal. All it needs is a smoke. Too bad you've already had your nightly cigarette."

He half smiled at me, showing one dimple. "What have *you* got?"

"The Meg Special."

"Eggs?"

"Sort of a Tex-Mex omelet. The Meg Special is different every day." I took a bite, chewed, and desperately needed to spit it out. I swallowed it and washed it down with coffee, which didn't really help.

"Tasty?" John asked.

"A little hot," I croaked.

"Need some water?"

"I can't ask for water," I whispered. "I have to be careful how I fix this. If I piss Purcell off, God knows what he'll serve to people for the rest of the night." I motioned to Purcell, and he walked over from the grill. I smiled. "How much cayenne you using?"

"A half."

My Lord, half a teaspoon of cayenne pepper in two eggs. No wonder. "I like it, but it may be too spicy for the clientele. Let's try an eighth."

Purcell nodded curtly and started to turn away.

"Water, please," John called. He muttered to me, "Thirsty tonight."

Purcell brought John a glass of water. When Purcell went back to the grill, John nodded to the glass.

Watching Purcell out of the corner of my eye, I drank half the glass and slid it back to John. "Thanks," I breathed.

"Experimenting on the customers?"

"I told him an eighth before I left. He just forgot."

"Why don't you write it down?"

"He can't read." I took a huge bite of egg to get rid of it more quickly, then a swig of coffee and another long drink of John's water. "I try to work with him because he's a good employee. Shows up. My parents don't understand this."

"Are you going to stay here after high school and run the restaurant with them?" John took a bite of his blessedly mild food.

I laughed. "Hell no. I'm gone the night of June seventh, after graduation. I'm not even staying around for the party. And that's saying a lot, for me to pass up a party."

He swallowed. "You know this town so well. Better than *I* do, even. This place is yours. That's a really good reason to stay."

Funny, I'd never felt claustrophobic at the Elvis table before. I looked around the diner. Maybe it was the jukebox, humming low as it did when no one put in a quarter for a song. Maybe the low hum made me nervous.

But my gaze came to rest on John, and I knew *he* was making me nervous. Chatting to me like he was talking to a dead girl. Trying to trap me here.

I said quickly, "It's a better reason to leave."

"You don't feel any loyalty to your parents? Don't you want to stay here and help them out?"

"I've helped them out plenty. They make me work here, and they don't pay me. It's basically slave labor. Kind of like following *you* around."

He went back to eating like my snark didn't concern him. But he looked hurt. Those worry lines appeared between his eyebrows. I couldn't resist him when a little bit of boy showed through the tough exterior.

I lowered my voice. "They don't need my help. They just pretend to need my help so they can keep me close. They're overprotective. It'll drive you crazy. It honestly will."

"Overprotective, why?" he asked without looking up from his plate. "Only child?"

"Beats me. Anyway, they say they need me, but they don't. They'll hire somebody, just like they hired people to fill in this week while they're out of town." I took my last hell-bite.

"What if you leave and they go out of business? Won't you feel like it's your fault? Oh." He put down his fork. "I didn't mean to upset you."

"It's the pepper, John." I drained his water, then sniffed and dabbed at my eyes with a paper napkin from the holder. "Of course I won't feel like it's my fault. It's the biggest kindness I can do them. If they can't run a restaurant by themselves, they need to go back to selling vinyl siding. I can't do it for them. We'd always be dependent on each other and always unhappy, feeling pressured and letting each other down."

"Mmph. What are you going to do when you grow up, then?"

I glared at him. "Nice. I got a tuition scholarship to UAB."

He put his fork down again. "*You?* Got a *scholarship?*"

"It's not a scholarship for good grades," I assured him. "It's a scholarship for having two loser parents who can hardly keep a diner out of bankruptcy."

"For a needs-based scholarship, you still have to make good grades." He sat back and stared at me like he'd never seen a blue-haired girl before. "Don't worry. I won't tell anyone."

"Ha."

"But how are you going to pay for the rest of it? Room and board?"

"I'll find a job. Rent a cheap apartment on the Southside with a roommate or two."

He nodded. "Tiffany."

"I hadn't thought about it," I said. "That would involve planning and commitment."

"Right." He continued to look at me very seriously. "What are you going to major in?"

"Management, so I can run hotels and restaurants."

He laughed.

"What the hell's so funny? I enjoy doing this. I just don't want to do it *here*."

He laughed harder. "I'm sorry. I just can't imagine you managing anything." He kept laughing until he looked up and saw my face. "What."

"I've been keeping the books for this place since I was eleven years old." With a few months off when I was thirteen.

"Well, how was I supposed to know—"

"I just sat here and told you I got a scholarship to the university, and you act like I'm At Risk."

"If you would just tell me this stuff in the first place—"

"Why should I? I never intended to wow you with my credentials. You're the one who set out on this quest to save the children."

He drew himself up in his seat to look more threatening. "You would think someone in your position, in as much trouble as you're in, would try to make a better impression on the police."

"You would think." I couldn't remember why I'd had a crush on this ass. "In fact, I managed just fine until you showed up at that bridge."

He gaped at me in disbelief. I felt myself cringe under that dark, hard gaze. "Meg, you were drunk, stoned, letting Eric Wexler feel you up, and five minutes from getting hit by a train."

I rolled my eyes. "I suppose I should point out to you yet again that I did *not* get hit by a train. I made a mistake. If I turn in my proposal to the Powers That Be, everything will work out fine. I think you're scared to live life, and you're putting that on *me*."

"Just the opposite. You feel guilty for planning to leave town. You're trying to turn it around and make me feel like an idiot for staying."

"You're wrong," I said, because he was wrong. But now that he mentioned it, I *could* make him feel like an idiot for staying. "I looked you up in last year's yearbook, and I saw you were the ACT high scorer. I'm sure you were offered scholarships for that."

His steak suddenly needed his attention.

"Big-ass scholarships," I said. "You were captain of the state championship track team."

His vegetables also needed to be cut into small bites.

"It's pretty common for people to put off college for a year," I said. "You could still go to UAB and join the track team with your friends, and the university would give you your scholarship back.

Hell, with your *police academy* training, you could get a high-paying job as a security guard or a rent-a-cop while the rest of us are slaving away, waiting tables for rent."

"I have a job to do here," he muttered.

"What job? Your weird compulsion to protect and serve? You could do that anywhere. Why does it have to be here?"

"This is my home."

"I thought you lived by yourself in an apartment. Is your family in town?"

He looked up. "You mean my wife, and my children who read manga?"

I felt myself blush. Good one. "I mean your parents."

He shook his head. "They got divorced when I was nine. My mom stayed in town for a few years after that, but finally she couldn't stand it anymore, and she split. She lives in Virginia. My dad wanted me to finish school where I started, so he stayed with me until I graduated. Then he split. He lives in Colorado."

"This diner is the closest thing you have to a home," I mused. "You're like a bachelor homesteader on the prairie who eats all his meals in town."

"If I were a bachelor homesteader on the prairie, I'd know my way around a cast-iron skillet and some fatback." He was looking down at his plate, but his dimples showed as he smiled at himself.

"Your friends are gone, your family's gone, and you're not living in the house where you grew up. What makes this town your home? What do you have left here? Just the bridge?"

His dimples faded.

"Let's just say, hypothetically, that you went to UAB," I suggested. "Would you major in criminal justice?"

"No. What a waste."

This surprised me, considering how into this cop life he was. Then I thought I'd hit on it. Aim higher. "Pre-law?"

"No. Getting people on that end doesn't help. You major in criminal justice or law to learn to send them to jail as cost-effectively as possible and keep them from killing each other while they're there. But they spend their time in jail learning how to commit bigger and better crimes. Why bother?"

"What would you major in, then?"

"I'm not going to college, so it doesn't matter."

"Hypothetically, hello."

Between bites he said, "Art."

My jaw dropped. "Art!"

"That's what everybody says to me. And that's another reason not to go to college. You can't make a living if you major in art."

"Some people do, if they try hard enough. It was just the farthest thing from my mind for you." For a few moments, I watched him eat. Officer After in the dark blue uniform—I couldn't see him as an art major. He would think art was for sissies. But Johnafter jogging in the park? Maybe. Johnafter from Spanish class? Definitely.

I said, "You could at least work as a cop and do art on the side, and feel more fulfilled because you'd studied what you wanted to study. If you don't, you'll always be bitter toward your wife and your children who read manga. You'll always wish you'd gotten out and lived life when you had the chance." I lowered my head, trying to catch his eyes, which were still focused on his food. He wouldn't look at me. "Why art?"

He attacked his steak with his knife again. "That's the way to move people, to change people, and prevent them from hurting each other and themselves. Art is the most effective form of communication. You can use it to lift the human spirit, and make people realize there's more to life than their next meth high." He took a bite, chewed slowly, looked up at me, swallowed. "What's the matter?"

I realized I was gaping at him. "Nothing." I shut my mouth.

"Oh, I'm sorry. I forgot that cops are supposed to be stupid."

"I never said you were stupid."

"You don't need a college education to be a cop. You just have to be able to drive. Read. Write. Or not." He was quoting back what I'd said that first night at the bridge.

"Well, excuse me for making a rude comment when you had just *arrested* me!" As Purcell leaned over the table with the coffeepot, I said, "Waiter, this is not the policeman I ordered. I wanted one with a lot less sauce."

Purcell filled both mugs and turned away. "Your folks don't pay me enough for this."

John watched Purcell retreat to the grill. Then he leaned across the table toward me. He said quietly, "I'm not going to college. All you're doing is making me dissatisfied with my lot in life."

I leaned forward, too, and whispered like this was a big secret.

"Your lot in life? A lot is something you draw, like straws. It's chance. You didn't get this life by chance. You chose it on purpose. If you're dissatisfied with it, you can change it."

"I'm not dissatisfied." He leaned back and raised his voice to a normal level, as if he'd flicked a switch. "So, you want to major in business so you can manage a restaurant that isn't your parents' restaurant."

I sighed and let him change the subject. It was a wonder I'd gotten all that out of Dudley Do-Right in the first place. "Yeah, and not your local Applebee's, either. I want to experience exotic locales."

"Exotic locales. Like what?"

"I wouldn't know. I've never been to an exotic locale. I was *supposed* to go to one for the first time over spring break." Like I said, it was a lot easier for me to take potshots at him when he was in uniform.

Rather than biting, he took a bite of broccoli.

I went on, "From watching the Travel Channel, I'd say the place in the world I'd most want a job is Key West, Florida. It looks so cool. A tropical paradise. The southernmost point in the United States, south of Miami even. And they seceded from the union. In 1982, they declared themselves a separate country from America. Did you know that?"

"Yes."

"It didn't work, though."

"No."

"No one took them seriously."

"Imagine."

I was a little irked at him for making fun of my tropical paradise. "Have you been there?"

"No."

"Have you ever been anywhere?"

He looked hurt again. "Of *course* I've been somewhere. Just because I'm a cop—"

"Oh, don't start with that again. I've never been anywhere, so I don't assume. Where did you go?"

"All over Europe. France, Portugal, Spain, Italy, Switzerland, Austria, Germany, Denmark, the Netherlands, Belgium, Luxembourg." He traced his route in the air with his finger. "I rode the Eurail and stayed in hostels."

"God, you're kidding! When?"

"A few months ago. I graduated from the police academy in November, but I couldn't take this job until I turned nineteen in December. I needed something to do for a month. Something other than hang out here."

"I am *so* jealous," I said, meaning it.

"Well. I saved up my salary for this while I was at the police academy. I figured it might be my one chance to see the world, since I'll be in this town working for the rest of my life."

"Oh." What a buzz-kill. While I was at it, I decided to push the buzz-kill further. It would help me get over my crush on him. "Did Angie go with you?"

"She'd be scared to do something like that. Anyway, she broke up with me right before then."

I couldn't resist. "Small wonder. You're a regular barrel of monkeys."

He put down his fork on his empty plate and gave me the look.

I decided this was a good time to finish my lunch. I popped the last of the corn bread into my mouth and wished desperately that the Meg Special came with more meat so I'd have something else to do. He was still giving me the look. I could feel it singeing my hair.

Finally I gave in and glanced up at him, and almost flinched backward with the force of his angry dark eyes.

"*God*, Meg!"

"Well, now it's my turn to backtrack," I said. "I didn't mean that like it sounded."

"How else could you have meant it?"

"I didn't know you still had the hots for Angie."

"I don't. But *you* don't know that. You're really going out of your way. The whole time we've sat here, you've been feeling around for a soft spot to stab me." He closed his eyes, sighed through his nose, opened his eyes. "Do you *hate* me?"

"I have good reason to hate you, John. You arrested me and ruined my spring break on purpose." I tapped my knife on my plate. "No, I don't hate you. But you're not exactly innocent here. An hour ago at the crime scene, you were giving me all kinds of Sullen Malarkey."

Ever so slowly, the look melted into two friendly, smiling eyes. "Sullen— You were touching the evidence."

"You were mad at me because Will pulled my hair. Come on."

He glanced through the windows at the cop car in the parking lot. "The night is young. Let's get back to work. Truce." He extended his hand across the table for me to shake. "Friends. Partners, for three and a half more nights."

I put my hand close to his, then pulled away. "I can't touch you while you're in uniform."

"For you, I'll make an exception."

What the hell did *that* mean? While the possibilities circled in my brain, I touched his wrist with my fingers. His hand clasped over my wrist, then slid back to my palm. His thumb grazed the back of my hand. There was no shaking, just tentative touching of hands.

This was like no handshake I'd ever shared. Clumsy, and sexy, and way too friendly for comfort.

Friends my ass.

10

"Something bad is going to happen here," Tiffany said.

Something already had. This was my third time riding along on John's graveyard shift, and this was the third wreck at the Birmingham Junction in as many nights.

Tiffany and I sat on the back bumper of the ambulance with the doors open behind us. Normally the too-familiar smell of hospital disinfectant would have driven me away. But I was tired, and there was nowhere else to sit and watch the paramedics treat minor injuries.

At least, I assumed Tiffany watched the paramedics as they eased an old man onto a stretcher and shone a penlight into his eyes. Personally, I watched John. He looked so hot standing in a circle of broken glass, directing traffic around two cars crushed together and two tow trucks easing into place to carry them away.

The flow of traffic kept drifting toward John. Once he even had to jump out of the way to avoid getting hit. Probably the drivers were distracted by how hot he was. I wondered if I should tell him this for his own safety. Let Officer Leroy direct traffic.

"They didn't even bother with the fire truck for this one," Tiffany said. "They brought the fire truck last night because that wreck was worse. The paramedics told me this is the most dangerous intersection they've ever seen."

"More importantly," I said, "was Brian on the fire truck last night?"

"Yes. He told me not to call him anymore." She still stared at the paramedics, but she blinked more rapidly, fighting off tears.

"The Silent Treatment," I muttered. Honestly, I thought it was for the best. Brian wasn't good enough for Tiffany. But there was no way Tiffany would believe that. And I hated to see her unhappy.

Luckily, we were distracted just then from the subject I'd stupidly brought up. My paramedic friend Quincy came back to the ambulance. He cuffed me on the shoulder and wagged his gray eyebrows at me. "Hey there, tiger. I bet you're enjoying riding around with the cops. Top speed and making noise. Right up your alley."

"Aren't *you* all daffodils and fluffy bunnies for springtime," I said. "Why were you so mean to me at the bridge last week?"

"You were trying your best to kill yourself after I worked so hard to keep you alive four years ago. Let me 'splain something to you. Here's thirteen, and here's seventeen." Blue veins showed through his weathered skin as he held his left fist low and his right fist high. He traced an imaginary line up diagonally with his finger. "You're supposed to mature." He grabbed a medical kit from inside the ambulance and sauntered back toward the wreck.

"Ha," I called after him. It was hard to think of a snappy comeback when he was right. Then I murmured, "At least I've matured in taste."

Tiffany sang quietly, "You like Johnafter, you like Johnafter."

"He's easy on the eyes." I liked his *halt* motion to cars. My favorite, though, was his *what are you waiting for* motion, waving curtly beside his ear. "But nothing will come of it."

"If anyone could date the cop who arrested her, it would be you."

"Thanks, Tiff."

"Why won't anything come of it? Would he get in trouble?"

"I don't think so," I said. "Not after I turn in my Goody Two-shoes proposal to the Powers That Be and John's no longer the boss of me. And I'm sure before we did anything, he'd okay it with the chief of police, and fill out some forms in quadruplicate. But there's the pesky detail that he doesn't like me very much."

She made a *nuh-uh* noise just like John's friends had the night before at McDonald's.

"Did he have his hand on my ass?" I asked.

"Uh, no. But between cars, he keeps looking over here at you."

I turned my head toward her, to fake John out. Then I cut my eyes at him.

He was staring at me, all right. And when he saw I'd noticed, he didn't try to hide it. He grinned at me.

Maybe my ploy had worked. I wore a respectable shirt that buttoned down the front, only—whoops!—I must have forgotten to fasten the button over my cleavage. No respectable girl would wear her shirt open that low. (Cough.)

Also, just before the shift started tonight, I had walked to the drugstore across the street from Eggstra! Eggstra! and used one of their perfume testers. Nothing too obvious or flowery, just a body spray with a hint of musk that said you admired your captor.

He was wearing cologne again, too, which meant at the very least he didn't go home and throw away all his toiletries in horror after I told him he smelled good. I hoped the two of us together didn't smell too overpowering to other people, like we were trying to attract water buffalo.

By now the tow trucks had lumbered away with their loads of broken car. John pointed at me to get my attention. He circled his finger in the air to tell me to wrap it up, then pointed to his cop car.

I made a series of baseball catcher's signs.

He smiled. Cocked his head toward his car.

I gave him a thumbs-up.

"You're right," Tiffany said. "I don't think he likes you very much."

I couldn't help smiling myself. Then I felt the smile fade. "Anyway, it wouldn't work out. I'm leaving, and he's staying."

"It might work out."

"It can't." Catching a whiff of disinfectant from the ambulance, I jumped down from the bumper and walked to John's car. The night wind turned bitter, and I shivered in my jacket.

I opened the passenger door of the cop car and was about to sit down when something stopped me in mid-sit. John was reading my notebook.

Without looking up at me in alarm, without looking up from the notebook at all, he said, "Got a call from Lois. We need to head to Martini's to break up a fight."

I sat down slowly and closed the door. *He was reading my notebook.* Since our talk last night, we'd gotten along great. Because of the truce. Or because we understood a little more about each other, like a beam of sunlight shining into the dark night shift.

And now this!

In my mind, I reviewed all the phrases in the notebook. Should I snatch it from him? This would save me if he hadn't gotten very far in his reading. It would also expose how embarrassing the notebook was to me. Or should I play it cool? Ostensibly the notebook was information for my Goody Two-shoes proposal. It embarrassed me only because it was information about him, and I was falling hard.

The snatch won out. "Give me that," I said, grabbing for the notebook.

He held it away from me, over his head, and gave me a cocky grin and one dimple.

My heart rushed through a beat. What was this, middle school? "That's mine."

"It's evidence."

It certainly was.

He lowered the notebook and studied it against the steering wheel. "It's a haiku."

"Do I look Japanese to you?"

"I've told you, yes."

"Wrong number of syllables on each line."

He ran his finger along a line, counting aloud.

"It's just a collection of weird things you say," I explained.

He gasped in mock outrage. "You told me you were taking notes for the project you're proposing."

"I am, in a roundabout way. My project has to do with you."

He handed the notebook back to me. I sat on it. Then he started the car and nodded downward so I knew to flick the switch for the siren.

As we accelerated across town, his grin didn't fade, just hardened into place. "Tell me about your project."

"It's a surprise," I said loudly over the siren.

"I don't like surprises."

No surprise there.

"I'm interested in this transformation you went through so quickly to become a cop," I said. "You don't have the heart of a cop."

"Do, too."

"But you do and say things that make you appear to be a cop, and that fool everybody. For instance, the fact that no one can touch you while you're in uniform."

"That's a safety issue. I'm carrying a gun. People hugging you or even touching you casually could pull out your weapon or set it off."

"Set it off? Don't you have the safety on or whatever so no one gets shot accidentally?"

"You can't be too careful with weapons. Also, when you go to a scene, especially a domestic, suspects want to approach you and get you on their side. You can't let them touch you. You maintain a buffer zone around yourself, which makes you more threatening. It's another safety issue."

"It's a safety issue, and you enjoy being threatening."

We went airborne over the speed bump downtown, but this time I didn't think to wake the dead with my *Dukes of Hazzard* yell. My eyes were on John.

"I like being respected," he said. "I didn't get a whole lot of respect when I was a skinny high school kid. And I like that people don't question me." He glanced at me. "Until now."

"Why don't you want people to ask you questions?"

"I guess I feel like I don't have very good responses."

"Responses," I repeated. "See there? That's another thing you do. You use words that distance you from what you're talking about. *Responses* instead of *answers*. *Vehicles* instead of *cars*. *Weapons* instead of *guns*. What do you call these?" I touched my jeans.

"Denim trousers."

"What do you call this?" I touched a demure part of my shirt.

"Chemise."

I put my hands up to my face. "This?"

"Visage."

I touched my hair.

He turned off the main road, onto the dirt road through the woods that led to Martini's. Yes, everything in this town was at the end of a dirt road through the woods.

He looked over at me. "Indigo," he said. "Cyan." He glanced at the road in front of him, glanced at me. He reached over and ran his fingers down one of the darkest strands in the back, where I'd used a little purple. "Violet."

The car had gotten very warm. I slipped off my jacket. He gave me one more sideways glance, but I couldn't tell whether it was for my violet hair or my cleavage.

"Hey," he said, "I got the day off—I mean the night off—for Rashad's party."

"You're kidding!"

"Nope. Normally I'd be off Thursday and Friday and come back to work on Saturday. But this week I'll be off Thursday, work Friday, and be off Saturday. Thank you!" He gestured out the windshield as if paying homage to the Powers That Be who let him switch his schedule. And then he turned to me again. "Thank you."

"No prob." Before this, I'd entertained a miniature thought of what might happen if I saw John when my official punishment was over two nights from now. This small thought had not become a large thought because it had no room to grow. Currently John was pouring Miracle-Gro on the thought. I was just getting out the hedge clippers to cut the thought down when he parked in front of Martini's.

The town's only non-country bar was as disappointing as everything else around here. With a name like Martini's, you would expect an upscale place like you'd find at Five Points in Birmingham, with low blue lighting and a mod interior. Well, I'd never seen the inside, but the outside was cement block, and I could use my imagination. They probably couldn't mix a martini. Or if they could, they served it to you in a beer mug.

The gravel parking lot was packed with cars. John parked near the dirt road for quick access if he had to chase a drunk driver. I knew John. But then he sat in the car with the siren still screaming, while the bar's patrons peeked out the entrance and ducked back inside.

"Are you scared?" I asked.

"Of course," he said, watching the entrance. "If you didn't feel the fear, going alone into a bar fight, you'd be stupid. Or insane. Or perhaps just gravely ill-informed. That's not why I'm waiting, though. I'm letting the siren soften everyone up." He reached down and flicked off the siren switch. In the siren's place, a bass line throbbed from the bar. "Back in a flash."

"I'll go in with you and protect you."

He groaned. "I knew you'd say that. I'm serious, Meg. I can't have you in there. I really don't think anything will happen. If I did, I'd call for backup before I went in. But you never know with that many people, most of them drunk. That's why they had a fight in the first place."

"How am I going to gather material for my haiku?"

"Look, it's dangerous enough when I'm worried about my own safety and the safety of everyone in there. I don't want to be worried about yours, too. It's distracting."

"Just stop worrying about me, then. I can take care of myself."

"I don't want you to get hurt," he said.

"Right. You'll get demoted to jail guard. I'm not buying it."

"No. *I* don't want you to get hurt." He put his hand on my knee. "Meg, please stay in the vehicle."

"Okay."

My knee radiated heat. As I watched him pull himself from the car and walk casually across the brightly lit parking lot, I thought dumb things: I will never wash my knee again. I will never wash these jeans again. I will cut the knee out of these jeans and sew a pillow to sleep on every night, just to have a molecule of him in my bed with me.

He slipped his nightstick from a loop in his belt and disappeared into the bar. The throbbing music stopped.

At least once a night, I watched him walk into danger. With his hand on his nightstick or his hand on his gun. It was like sitting up nights in your trailer, keeping the fruit cobbler warm in the oven, listening to the police scanner.

And I couldn't stand it. I was not cut out for sitting alone and still in the dark, waiting.

I forced myself to stand it. I prepared to wait long minutes before the shot rang out. Or until he staggered out the door with a knife in his back.

There was no wait at all. Almost immediately, people poured out of the bar like they were ants and John had stepped on their bed. Among them Eric, staggering as he led Angie Pettit by the hand across the parking lot and behind a pickup truck. Then the pickup truck turned on its headlights and drove away, revealing Eric's Beamer.

I watched them. The scene registered with me at some low level. Hmmm, what was that drunk wanker doing with the midget?

But any inkling of them was gone the second John appeared in the doorway of the bar, unshot, unstabbed, as casual and composed in his cop-like way as when he went in. I gripped the front of the seat with both sweaty hands to keep from jumping out of the car and running to him.

And then I got completely freaking furious with myself. I did hope that I was not entertaining a plot to somehow *date* John after? I cranked up the chain saw to cut down the plot made by Miracle-Gro.

He got back into the car with much clinking of the weaponry attached to his belt. "What's wrong? I guess you saw Eric and Angie."

Eric and Angie. Ha. I pressed one finger between my eyes, still concentrating on the chain saw. Feel the chain saw. *Be* the chain saw.

"You know it doesn't mean anything," John said kindly. "He only asked her out to get back at me."

"Did it work?" As if I were worried about *Eric* right now. The chain saw had run out of gas.

"No. I've known Eric for a long time. I expect that kind of thing from him. And Angie . . . It just seems bitchy, doesn't it?"

I straightened in my seat and shrugged halfheartedly. "I don't know anything about her except that she wears clothes made for Bratz."

He couldn't have been very jealous, because he didn't argue. Instead, he produced the ol' clipboard.

Eric sat behind the wheel of the Beamer now, with Angie in the passenger seat. But he was scared to make a move as long as John remained across the parking lot from him. "Aren't you going to walk over there?" I asked. "I know Eric won't go to jail for underage drinking, but at least you could get his parents to take away his TV privileges."

John crossed through some of his clipboard forms. "I think I'll call him and Angie over here. It's more intimidating to make them move instead of me going to them. They'll be standing up and we'll be sitting down, which is not what you want. You want to be higher than the suspects, talking down to them, if possible. But in this case"—he gestured to the official police equipment and the cracked vinyl interior—"the Crown Vic speaks for itself, don't you think?"

"Oh, yeah, it's got Authority written all over it." Old, tired, bitter Authority, stuck in this town.

John flashed his headlights and made a big motion with one hand. Eric easily could have pretended he didn't know John meant him in the crowded parking lot. But he didn't dare.

He *did* dare to open Angie's door for her (a gentlemanly

custom I'd had no idea he understood) and hold her hand again as they crossed the lot unsteadily.

John didn't watch them coming. He bent his head to the clipboard.

"What do you write in those forms?" I asked.

"Nothing. I just do this to look threatening."

I watched him scribble, and I made out his tiny drawing of a martini glass, with olive. It wasn't often that I got to study him like this, concentrating, in full light. He gently bit his soft bottom lip.

Maybe I was experiencing more Stockholm Syndrome. But that's not what it felt like. It felt like relief that he was alive, and joy that he was here in the car with me. I couldn't help showing him my appreciation. "You're sexy when you threaten people."

He turned to me. And oh oh oh, he gave me the look! Not the dark, threatening look, either. The dark, warm look I had imagined, as if he was in love with me.

But also wary.

Which was smart of him.

The worry lines appeared between his eyebrows. "Don't tease me," he said.

"I'm not teasing you."

He pointed at me with his pen. "I'm serious."

"So am I." I brushed some imaginary lint from my shirt, or touched my cleavage to catch his eye, depending on your perspective. "Are you afraid you'll be in trouble? I figure you'd be in trouble if we did something now. But not at 6:01 A.M. on Thursday, when my penance is over and you get off work."

"Thursday," he said thoughtfully. "What day is today?"

"Mon— It's after midnight. Tuesday."

As he checked his watch, Eric and Angie reached his side of the car. "Look bored," he told me.

Whatever!

He hit the switch to roll down his window. "Mr. Wexler. Ms. Pettit."

Eric nodded and slurred, "Officer After." Angie shrank behind Eric.

"You're both about a year and a half too young to be here." I loved listening to his calm authoritarian voice, when it wasn't directed at me.

"So are you," Eric said, but he didn't sound as cocky as he had at the bridge. Probably not quite as drunk.

"It's my job to be here," John said. "I come here just about every night to break up a fight, between, oh, eleven forty-five and—" He turned to me. "What would you say?"

"Twelve fifteen."

"Twelve fifteen," he agreed, turning back to Eric. "So keep that in mind the next time you're thirsty. In the meantime, you're not driving home drunk. You need to call your daddy to come get you. And Angie, if you're not riding with Eric's daddy, you need to call your own daddy."

Angie stepped from behind Eric. In her cute pipsqueak voice, she asked, "Can't *you* take me home?"

If she batted her eyelashes, I was going to get out of the car and slap her.

"It's a law enforcement vehicle, not a taxi," John said.

I pressed a hand to my mouth to suppress a burst of laughter, then acted like I was clearing my throat.

Eric leaned down to give me the evil eye through the open window. I half expected him to call me a stupid bitch. But such things did not happen when you were allied with Officer After.

"Got your cell phone?" John prodded Eric. "Let's see you call your pop."

"What if I don't want to do that?" Eric asked.

John bent over his clipboard again. Holding it so only I could see it, he quickly drew an amazingly accurate little Eric face with its tongue sticking out. "My shift ends at six A.M.," he said without looking up. "I can sit here and watch you until then. Turn the ignition over and I've got you." He rolled up the window.

Eric took the hint. He led Angie back across the parking lot to the Beamer, weaving a little. He held his head high and swung her hand, trying to save face. But there wasn't any face to save. I smiled.

"God," John said. "She's acting like she's trying to make me jealous or get back at me. And then she asks if I can take her home. Why would she do that? I'm telling you, *she's* the one who broke up with *me*."

I didn't like this turn in the conversation. I wanted to get back to the beautiful, dark look he'd given me. But if he was interested in Angie, well . . . A blue-haired girl didn't have a chance against a midget girl, or a dead girl, either. You gotta box your weight. "She wants you back," I said.

"*I* don't want *her*. She was very decided and very detailed when she explained why she didn't want me anymore last fall. I'm sure this will pass. College must not be working out for her."

"What's her major?" If it was something other than early childhood education, she probably *was* in trouble.

"Crap."

Now I *did* burst into laugher. I kept my eye on Eric and Angie in the Beamer across the lot and hoped they'd think I was having another coughing fit.

"Bitchy crap," John added.

There was no disguising the laughter now, and even John was grinning at me. Gasping, I said, "She's majoring in bitchy crap? Well, that's just silly."

John straightened his shoulders and his face. "You can't make a living if you major in bitchy crap."

That was it. We both let go. Angie's punishment was the knowledge people were laughing at her.

I couldn't leave it alone, could I? Into the laughter, I asked, "Why'd you start dating her in the first place? Because she'd do you?"

Dimples still showing, John sniffed and rubbed the tears away from his eyes. He nodded toward Eric. "You would know. It goes a long way when you're seventeen. Obviously."

"Speaking of which," I said.

He rubbed his thumb back and forth slowly across his soft bottom lip. "Where were we? 6:01 A.M. on Thursday, huh?"

I grinned.

He swallowed. "What exactly are we talking about?"

"Oh, no. You're not entrapping me. I've watched prostitution stings on *Cops*. I won't be the first one to mention the sex act."

Under his dark blue uniform, his chest rose and fell rapidly. I wished I dared put my hand there to feel how his heartbeat sped up. It was nothing compared with mine. I could hardly believe my luck. I had a crush on a cop, and for some unknown reason, he crushed on me right back. I, blue-haired girl-felon, was seducing Officer After.

"I've been through this before with Angie, remember?" he said. "She left town and dumped me. This would be the same. Wouldn't it?"

"Not if there were no strings attached," I said.

Oh, the gentle lip-biting. "I'm not sure I can function with no strings attached."

"Try it. You'll like it. Just once. Get it out of your system."

He sat back against the vinyl seat and gazed across the parking lot at the Beamer. "I think it might be a disaster."

"I think it would be perfect," I said truthfully.

He passed his fist across his clean-shaven jaw, then picked up his pen and busied himself scribbling on the clipboard. "6:01 A.M. on Thursday, then. Write that down in your notebook, and we'll call it a plan."

11

He let me drive! It took him until night four, but he let me drive!

Well, only for a few minutes.

And only a few feet.

And not the police car.

A March storm had blown up, soaking the cold night with rain. A car skidded off the slick road at the Birmingham Junction and got stuck in the muddy shoulder.

While the driver pressed on the gas, John threw his weight onto the back bumper. The tires spun, and the car didn't budge.

I got out of the cop car to help, despite the rain. Not that I really expected to be of assistance. But it was better than waiting around for John, making him fruit cobbler in my mind. He signaled the driver, and we both pressed our weight against the back bumper.

At least, that's what I thought. I pushed as hard as I could, and the tires spun. Then I looked over at John.

He was standing up. Staring at my ass. Now that he called my attention to it, I *did* feel a draft where my jacket rode up as I bent over. He was staring at the tattoo on my lower back of a bird escaping from a cage. That tattoo had cost me months of tips. The artist charged me extra because getting a tattoo at under eighteen was illegal without my parents' consent.

I straightened and put my hand on my back. I hoped John wasn't considering a sting operation on a Birmingham tattoo studio. It was out of his jurisdiction.

No . . . he was considering 6:01 A.M. Thursday. He focused on my hand where he'd seen my tattoo a moment before. Slowly his eyes moved up my body to meet my eyes. He blinked against the rain and remembered he was On Duty.

Then he squinted at the driver. "This is too distracting. Go trade places with that guy. It's *his* Goddamn car."

So I slipped into the driver's seat and watched in the rearview mirror for John's signal. When he pointed at me, I stomped the gas. The tires spun, then caught. The car shot forward. I checked the mirror again. The driver was wet with rain but otherwise spotless. John, plastered with mud, wiped dirt from his mouth with his sleeve.

The driver happily skidded away. Back in the cop car, John blew mud out of his nose with a Kleenex from the trunk. "I hate to go home and change with less than two hours left in the shift. What do you think?" He sneezed.

"If I were a criminal—and I am *not*—I wouldn't find you very intimidating right now. I would find you bedraggled."

"'Nuff said."

His apartment was in one of those complexes with twenty buildings, all the same, that had sprung up along the interstate. They housed people who worked at the car factory here in town but didn't want to commute from Birmingham. That is, people with no life.

It was only a minute's drive from the Birmingham Junction. Why, he could probably hear the car crashes from his patio. He definitely could hear the drone of the interstate. I heard it as soon as he pulled into a space and turned off the engine.

We sat there in silence, except for that hum of distant eighteen-wheelers, for ten seconds.

"Should you come in?" he asked.

"Why not? You don't want me to see your apartment?"

"It's not that. Somehow it just doesn't seem appropriate."

"I'm going to see it at 6:01 A.M. Thursday anyway. Unless you want to do it behind the storage buildings."

In the dim lights of the parking lot, I couldn't see him blushing. But I could *hear* him blushing as his breaths came more quickly.

"Yeah," he said, "but that's twenty-four hours from now."

I looked at my watch. "Twenty-five."

He pulled my wrist toward him and looked at my watch himself. Which sent sparks shooting down my arm, because he could have looked at his own watch. He chose to touch me instead.

136

"And forty-seven minutes," he said so close to my shoulder that I felt the low notes of his voice vibrate through me. "But if you stay in the car, I'll have to leave the keys so you can keep the heat on. And now that I've let you behind a steering wheel once tonight, I'm afraid you'll go for a joyride."

I smiled and winked at him.

"Come on in."

I expected his apartment to have walls, carpet, and kitchen tile the color of masking tape, as virgin as the day he moved in. Or little touches of homeyness, calico curtains and cookie-scented candles, left by the cobbler-baking phantom wife. This is not what I got. The living room was a gallery. Bold drawings crowded the walls, some framed, most tacked up bare.

My first thought was shock at what cool taste he had. My second thought was wonder at how he paid for actual drawings by actual artists. My third thought was suspicion the drawings were all by the same artist. They were similar in style, somewhere between photographic realism and manga. And similar to the little sketches in the margins of Johnafter's Spanish homework, *perro, sombrero, corazón.*

"You can draw!" I exclaimed.

"Yeah," his voice echoed from the kitchen.

"I mean *really* draw, like a professional. How can we claim to call a truce, and be friends, and plan for 6:01 A.M. Thursday, when you're hiding this whole other side of yourself from me?"

"I told you I would major in art, hypothetically."

"Yeah, but I thought the bullshit you fed me about lifting up the human spirit was compensation for not being able to draw."

He laughed.

I took a couple of steps over so I could lean around the kitchen doorway and see his dimples. "What do you use? Is this chalk?"

"Oil pastel, and some pencil."

"Instead of paint?"

"More control." He had taken off his muddy boots and stood in his socks by the sink. He reached up his pants leg, unstrapped a gun in a holster, and slid it onto the kitchen table. Then he ran the edge of his hand down his pants leg and threw the mud in the garbage can.

"No matter how careful you are," I said, "there's going to be a mess, and you're going to have to clean it up afterward."

"Mmph," he said, scraping off more mud.

I began beside the kitchen and moved around the living room, examining each drawing. Every one was a treasure of color and penciled detail. I could have stared at each of them for hours, but I felt like I had to hurry and get them all in. I would be back here at 6:01 A.M. sharp tomorrow morning, at which point I would be busy doing something else. And after that, I would never come back.

The drawings were like a map of his trip through Europe. There was the pyramid at the Louvre, the Matterhorn, and beach after beautiful beach that could have been anywhere on the Mediterranean. People stood in the foreground with their backs turned, enjoying the view. People, punctuated with the occasional green alien, or an elephant wearing a hat.

Strange that all this was hiding in that dark blue uniform.

In it, or behind it.

I made the entire circuit of the room, came even with the kitchen again, and stopped short in front of my favorite drawing so far. Venice, judging from the canal boats and the colorful buildings. A boy and a girl, too distant for details, stood in the middle of a bridge over the canal. But just to one side of them, the drawing dissolved into blank paper.

"That's one of my favorites," John said from the kitchen. "I hate that I couldn't finish it. The street flooded at high tide, and I had to move."

I nodded like I knew all about the streets flooding at high tide in Venice when you were trying to finish your drawing.

The last frame in the room, beside the front door, wasn't a drawing but a large photo of a family of four, with clothes and hair that would have been fashionable in the late nineties. Printed in black and white, the way people displayed photos that were really special. Blonde mother, dark father. The blond little boy with the dark eyes was John. The blond teenager with longish hair must have been his brother. Other than light eyes, he looked more like John than John.

"Does your brother live here in town?" I asked.

Water ran in the kitchen. John was washing his hands. He dried them on a towel and looked at them.

"John?"

He washed his hands again.

I used my best guilt-ridden murderess voice. "Out, damned spot! Out, I say!"

"*Macbeth*. Tenth grade." He dried his hands.

"Does your brother live here in town?" I repeated.

"No, he left." He unbuckled his gun belt and laid it on the kitchen table beside the holster from his leg.

"Can I touch it?" I crossed the living room, into the kitchen, and peered at the guns in their holsters. "Do you think I'll shoot you?"

He watched me with an amused smile. "Actually, I was thinking I should show you some basics, as part of your education this week. Or in case I get knocked out in the next twenty-five hours, and you're left in the vehicle with an unconscious police officer and a loaded weapon."

I hadn't expected him to agree. "You can't be too careful with guns," I reminded him.

He picked up one of the pistols and showed me some basics anyway. How to take out the clip of bullets, and how to check for a bullet in the chamber. He seemed to be concentrating on the gun. But there was no way he missed the way my hands shook on the table as he went through these motions so familiar to him.

I didn't want to see his sympathetic look for a frightened girl. I hated myself for being frightened.

He offered the gun to me, with the muzzle pointed toward himself. "No bullets," he said. "Safe."

I held out my shaking hand, and he placed the gun in my palm.

"Heavy," I said. Foreign. Strange to hold it in my hand. Warm from his body.

I held it as long as I could stand it, then offered it back to him—with the muzzle pointed toward the door, not myself. "Okay, I'm through with it."

"So soon?" He took the gun gently back from me. *Click, click, pop,* and it was together again.

"I am full of fear."

"Of a gun?" He cocked his head to one side, watching me. His voice was honey as he guessed, "Of 6:01 A.M. Thursday."

I'd never been scared of sex. It was what might come after that terrified me, tethers tying me down here. I shivered.

He touched my shoulder. "God, here I am worried about what I look like to suspects when you're soaked, too. Come with me."

I followed him through the living room and into his bedroom. More drawings covered the walls. On his bedside table sat a police scanner, humming, occasionally crackling with Lois's voice.

He disappeared into his closet and brought out a long-sleeved T-shirt emblazoned with the words *To Protect and Serve.*

I took it from him. "Wow, I've crossed over."

He disappeared again and brought out another leather cop jacket.

I took it. "Does this mean we're going steady?"

He gave me the one-dimpled smile before looking in the closet once more for a clean, pressed uniform on a hanger. "Be right back." He walked into the bathroom and closed the door.

I could have secreted myself in the closet to change. But since I was me, I shed my wet jacket and shirt there in his bedroom. I paused just a few moments in the hope he would (gasp!) catch me in my bra. But even if that happened, that's all that would happen, because it was not yet 6:01 A.M. Thursday, and John went By The Book. I pulled on his warm, dry shirt and jacket.

I started my circle around this new room of the art gallery. One of the first drawings I came to was of the Devil fountain at Five Points, with several of the animal statues coming to life and wearing hats. Then more angles of the artsy section of Birmingham, ornate mansions next door to dilapidated apartment buildings.

And then, across from his bed, right where he could see it first thing when he woke up each morning (or afternoon), was a large drawing of the bridge.

With no green aliens in it, no hat-wearing animals. No people.

Just the bridge, a stark shape against the too-blue sky.

He burst from the bathroom. At least, you would think he had, the way I jumped back from the drawing.

While he stepped into clean boots, I crossed to the dresser like nothing had happened, uncapped a bottle of cologne, and sniffed. That wasn't it. I picked up another. That wasn't it, either. If his scent of cologne was really laundry detergent or deodorant or even aftershave, I would be disappointed.

He reached past me for the last bottle and handed it to me. "It's this one."

I unscrewed the top and wet my finger with cologne. I half thought he would kick me out of his apartment, never to return, not even at 6:01 A.M. Thursday, for what I did next. I did it anyway. I reached up to touch his neck. Sliding my hand past his dark collar, I rubbed my finger across his collarbone.

He looked down at me and put his big, warm hand over my hand.

The scanner buzzed to life with Lois's voice. John didn't move, but those worried creases appeared between his eyebrows.

"I don't understand Lois's code," I whispered. "What is it?"

He dropped his hand and stepped away from me. Picking up my soaked clothes from the floor, I followed him into the living room, where he was already putting on his gun belt. "A fatality at the Birmingham Junction," he said. He bent to strap the other gun onto his leg. "What we've been waiting for."

I trailed him through the wake of his cologne. Out the door, into the fog that had replaced the rain, down the stairs, and into the car. He radioed to Lois that we were close by and could respond to this call. Which didn't matter, because every siren in town was already wailing.

I drew the seat belt across my chest and fastened it like a good girl. The past few nights I'd gotten used to wearing it. I hardly ever felt faint. Now I was back to the panicky feeling. I knew what John had meant when he said we'd been waiting for this wreck. Finally, after holding their breath responding to crashes at the dangerous intersection, the emergency response personnel had the fatality they'd dreaded. It was The Big One. And John wanted me, Tiffany, and Brian to get an eyeful.

I was scared. And tired of being scared.

As he checked both ways for nonexistent traffic and pulled

onto the main road, I said, "My favorite drawing wasn't the one of Venice. It was the one of the bridge. *Your* bridge."

He took a deep breath and sighed through his nose: *Here we go again.*

"But the view you should draw isn't the view *of* your bridge," I went on. "It's the view *from* your bridge."

His jaw hardened. "That's illegal, as we've established."

"Sometimes breaking a rule is worth it. You're so obsessed with this bridge. Haven't you ever longed to see the view from the other side?"

He made one final turn, and the red and blue lights came into view, flashing long on the wet pavement. "Why are you doing this?" he asked so quietly that I could hardly hear him over the sirens.

"Because of what you're about to do to me."

It was a one-car crash. A circle of cop cars, fire trucks, and ambulances surrounded the car. It had crumpled against a round pillar holding up the interstate. "How do you even *have* a wreck like that?" I asked.

"Drunk. Poor judgment." He opened his door. "Come on."

Normally I would have jumped at the chance to get out of the cop car with him on a call. Brian and Tiffany were there already. They stood on either side of the mangled car, far apart from each other, both with their arms folded. But I hung back against the hood of the cop car, trying to tamp the panic down.

John crossed the accident scene and talked to a couple of firemen in their long coats with their helmets on and face shields down. He slid an engine enclosed in a cube-shaped metal frame off the fire truck and set it heavily near the wreck. The firemen screwed some hoses into the motor. They attached the other ends of the hoses to what looked like an enormous set of pliers.

Quincy the paramedic passed by me. I called out to him, "Are those the jaws o' life?"

"Yeah. A little late for the *life* part. You can see no one's in a huge hurry." He kept ambling on his way.

The jaws o' life engine started up with a racket, and the firemen set to work spreading open the collapsed space that used to be the car's front door. Broken glass and shards of metal flew into the air, bounced on the hood of the car, and cascaded to the pavement.

John beckoned me forward to the crumpled car.

My heart raced. My fingertips tingled. Red lights flashed behind my eyes. But I had to do what John said. If I didn't, I wouldn't put it past him to throw me in jail again, 6:01 A.M. or no 6:01 A.M. I took a few steps forward.

Brian put himself in my path. He shook his head at me. "Meg. You don't want to see this."

Behind Brian, John still motioned to me. He called, "Come on."

Brian walked over to John. "Don't make her." He put his hand against John's shoulder to stop him.

John flinched away. "Do *not* touch me while I'm in uniform," he shouted.

Brian ducked back.

John walked toward me, grasped my wrist, and pulled me. By now my face felt like a mask, with no blood pumping to my skin. I knew I was as good as gone, but I'd lost the strength to fight. I stumbled after him toward the wreck.

The noise from the jaws o' life was so loud, I didn't see how the firemen or anyone else could stand over here. It pulsed loud enough to hurt, like a motorcycle twice as big as mine with no muffler. I felt the concussion of every pulse in my chest, throwing the rhythm of my heartbeat off. As the scene collapsed into tunnel vision, the pulse of the engine melded into one long scream.

The interstate lights glared off the firemen's face shields so I couldn't see their expressions. They looked like aliens in space suits. At a signal from John, they backed away from the car to let us see inside.

She was twisted in a way the human body did not twist, in a very, very, very small space.

For me to hear him over the jaws o' life, John must have shouted. But in my head his voice sounded smooth and hollow and sinister, like a doctor in my hospital room after I'd been sedated.

"This is what I wanted you to see."

12

I wasted away. My flesh shrunk so quickly, I seemed to melt, to collapse in on myself. Through my transparent skin, my bones showed. I wiggled one finger back and forth, watching the bones grind together underneath.

THE AMMONIA LODGED IN MY NOSTRILS like two Q-tips.

I meant to cross my right hand to my left arm and pull out the IV. I missed, and my hand bounced off my shoulder. I slid my hand down my arm, feeling for the needle. No IV.

I sniffed more ammonia, trying to get it past the Q-tips and into my brain. I couldn't wake up. I couldn't open my eyes.

"Do not stick a needle in me," I mumbled. "Whatever you do,

do not start an IV. I would rather die, do you understand? Go ahead and let me die."

"You're not dying," came Tiffany's voice. "And you're crazy if you think they'd let me start an IV. I'm lucky I got to take your blood pressure. Which is very low, by the way, so don't sit up yet."

I took one more big whiff and sat up. Outside the open square of the back of the ambulance, John stood chatting with Officer Leroy and another cop and Quincy. John was smoking a cigarette.

Bastard.

Bastard!

I moved toward him.

Fell.

Off the ambulance?

Heard Tiffany shriek.

Found myself lying on my back on the wet highway, the shock of the fall still rippling through my muscles.

John lifted me under the arms and stood me up against the ambulance bumper. "Watch that first step. It's a doozy," he said around the lit cigarette hanging from his lip.

I shoved him. His chest was solid under the dark uniform, and he didn't budge. I shoved him again, as hard as I could, but only shoved myself back against the ambulance. I screamed at him, "I had cancer, you fuck!"

The other cops and Quincy crowded around. Suddenly I could see myself the way they saw me, a blue-haired girl screaming for no reason. I was about to get taken to jail for assaulting a police officer.

John's cigarette dropped onto the wet asphalt and steamed there. I didn't look up at him to see whether he was gaping at me and the cigarette had fallen out of his mouth, or he'd thrown the cigarette down on purpose. I didn't want to know whether I'd mortified him in front of his macho coworkers. I didn't care.

"I'm hitching a ride on the fire truck back to my motorcycle," I told the cigarette. "I've had enough of what you wanted me to see. I'm done for the night."

My legs wobbled underneath me as I staggered to the fire truck, but no one offered to help me, not even Tiffany or Brian. Keeping my head turned away from the wreck, I pulled myself into the roomy cab of the fire truck. I curled up like a cat next to the giant pliers from the jaws o' life. Which was probably a good thing. I would need them to extract me from this fix I'd wedged myself into with Johnafter.

I HAD CANCER, YOU FUCK.

I was so tired. I'd almost finished my daily five-mile run in the park. And I hadn't been to sleep yet. Well, except for a half-hour catnap in the front of the fire truck before the emergency response personnel dropped me off.

Even on my last leg, I managed a burst of energy, trying to outrun the memory of my own words.

I-had-can-cer-you-fuuuuuuuuuu—

Part of me wanted to take it back. I hadn't looked at John's face when I shouted at him. I hadn't seen the dark look of pain. But I could imagine. This macho pride thing was very fragile, I knew. I'd hit him where it hurt, in front of the older men he was trying desperately to be like.

Then I remembered the twisted body in the very small space of the mangled car, and I wanted to shove John harder.

Done. I reached the wall of handprints and walked around it to cool down. I half expected the ghost of Johnafter to round the bend toward me.

We hadn't met in the park since that first afternoon. One night I'd asked him whether he was trying to avoid seeing me there. He'd responded like the honest do-gooder he was. Sometimes he had to stay late at the police station to finish paperwork for the arrests he'd made and reports he'd taken that night. So he didn't get to bed until mid-morning. He was still asleep when I went running.

He ran later in the afternoon, when he woke up. I wasn't willing to stay later and lose sleep to see him, any more than he was willing to get up early and lose sleep to see me. I guess we both understood that our relationship was built entirely on witty repartee, and neither of us thought we could be witty on four hours of shut-eye.

Wait a minute—what was I thinking? *What* relationship? We probably didn't even have an appointment for sex anymore. John was gone, back into the yearbook from whence he sprung. And I didn't look forward to spending my last night on patrol with Officer After.

My cell phone rang.

"John!" I exclaimed, sprinting to my motorcycle at the edge of the parking lot and pawing through my bag. We'd exchanged numbers in case another suspect tried to bash the door of the cop car while John wasn't around. "Hello?"

"Hey!" Tiffany said. "I was afraid you'd be asleep, but you sound wide awake."

I tried not to huff out my disappointment. Wiping wet blue strands out of my eyes, I said, "I just finished my run."

"You're running this week, even with everything else going on?"

"Have to."

"Well? Do you have leukemia?"

I held the phone at arm's length and frowned at it. If Tiffany knew why I ran, I was even more transparent than I'd thought. I brought the phone back to my ear. "Not today."

"That's good. How about last night? Were you okay last night? I've never seen anyone that mad."

I kicked my handprint on the wall. "Thanks to John." I should have been kicking John's handprint, but it was too high.

"He went after you, you know. On your way to the fire truck, you looked like you were about to fall over those orange cones. But I called him back. I was afraid you'd hit him again and get in trouble."

"I'm a threat, all right." I felt my face flush at the thought of John coming after me. He cared, he cared! He cared so much that he made me faint on purpose! I was pathetic.

Tiffany cleared her throat. "Listen, I wanted your advice on something."

I laughed heartily. "Yeah, I'm a regular Dear Abby. Shoot."

"Brian still isn't speaking to me. He won't return my calls. But right before we went to the bridge, he had started hinting every other word that he and I should have sex—"

I knew what she was getting at. "No."

"—and he was trying to convince me to do it. But I didn't want to."

"No."

"Now, to get back together with him—"

"No."

"—I thought I might tell him I've changed my mind."

"Earth to Tiffany!"

"Why not?" she exclaimed. Translation: *If you can have sex with a drug offender, why can't I have sex with the salutatorian?*

"I could probably think of twenty reasons. Since I haven't slept today, I can think of only three. First, you don't want to get back together with someone who gives you the Silent Treatment."

"The Silent Treatment isn't so bad."

"Obviously it's driving *you* crazy. Second, you're trying to get drunk and have sex because everyone else is doing it. At least, you think everyone else is doing it, because they're bragging about it. But you need to do what's right for you."

There was silence on the other end of the line. I waited for her to thank me for my infinite wisdom. Instead, she said, "I thought I could count on your support. You wear a T-shirt that says *Peer Pressure*."

"Today I'm going to peer pressure you into not doing something rather than doing something. Look, I use protection when I have sex. It's over, and I never think much about it again. With you, it would be different. You would use a condom, it wouldn't break, and there would be no problems. The next day, you would go to the doctor to make sure you weren't pregnant and didn't have AIDS. You would go back every day for a month." I raised my voice over Tiffany's giggles. "Three years later, you would still be obsessing that you were having a delayed reaction. You might be pregnant and you might have AIDS. You would do everything you could to keep Brian from breaking up with you, because if he did, he might call your mama and tell her you weren't a virgin."

"Am I that obvious?" Tiffany asked.

"Yes. And I'm not saying that's a bad way to be. I could probably use a little obsessive worry in my life. It would make me more balanced."

I realized with a start that I'd been pacing madly up and down the parking lot, as if Tiffany's sex life really concerned me.

I walked back to my motorcycle and continued, "I'm saying *you* would not be comfortable with casual sex. Or whatever we're talking about here. The National Honor Society version of prostitution. When it's right, you won't have to call me to check. You'll know. And here's the third reason you shouldn't do it. Sex isn't that great."

She was quiet. "Touch My Body" played in the background, like she'd been psyching herself up. "Oh, come on."

"It's not."

"It's supposed to be no good the *first* time. I thought you were way past that."

I laughed shortly. "Thanks, Tiff. It's still no good."

"Then why are you doing it?" she shrieked.

A gust of wind made me shiver in my wet sweatshirt. "I want to make sure I've lived, in case I don't have a lot of life left."

"You told me you finished jogging and you don't have leukemia!"

"I'm always waiting for the other shoe to drop."

"That sounds a lot like obsessive worry," she said.

"About this particular thing."

"It's a pretty intense particular thing, Meg."

"Yeah, well, you're one to talk. Go ahead and proposition Brian, and I'll tell the whole school you're a beer-swilling slut-whore."

She hung up on me.

I was just stuffing the phone back into my bag when it rang again. I clicked it on. "Okay, you're not a slut-whore. If you're going to run with the big dogs, you have to learn to take a joke."

Silence on the other end of the line again. But no "Touch My Body."

My heart stopped. "John?" I asked.

"The other one," Eric said.

My heart beat again, slowly. "Oh, hey! I've been expecting your call. And I take back what I said about you not being a slut-whore."

"Right back at ya," he said. "Booty call."

"I ain't no hollaback girl."

"Yes, you are."

A cop car cruised slowly by the park. Not John, of course. Some lucky soul on day shift. But my heart stopped again for the split second before I realized it wasn't him.

I was far gone. And I needed to come back. Otherwise I'd end up like Tiffany, making sacrifices on a boy's behalf.

"Okay, I guess I am. I need some sleep first, though."

"Leave your motorcycle at the police station tonight," Eric said. "I'll pick you up there at nine, and I'll have you back at the beginning of John's shift—when—ten?"

It never took Eric long.

"I couldn't get any pot," he warned me. "I'll have some beer, though."

"Are you crazy?" A couple of elderly ladies speed-walking on the track in sequined workout suits turned to stare at me. I lowered my voice. "I can't drink beer and then ride around for eight hours with John."

"Then I guess we'll have to do it sober." I could almost hear Eric shudder as he hung up.

Me too.

THAT NIGHT, I WALKED TO THE drugstore across the street from Eggstra! Eggstra! and bought condoms. I always brought condoms. Eric was liable to forget them and not care. Somehow I had known this about him from the very beginning.

Then I rode my motorcycle to the police station, as we'd agreed. Eric was fifteen minutes late picking me up, as predicted. And he would be fifteen minutes late dropping me off again, so John was sure to be steamed.

That was Eric's plan, and it was good.

I didn't even say anything when he turned the Beamer onto the dirt road and parked in the clearing beside the bridge.

He cut the engine and turned to me. At least, it sounded like he turned to me. Clouds covered the moon and stars. With the engine and the dashboard lights off, the darkness was total and heavy.

"This time I want you to take all your clothes off," he said, "not just pull your pants down six inches."

His tone was light. But for some reason, I took the words as a warning. I needed to see the look on his face.

"That's not how I do it," I said.

"I want you to do it my way this time."

"What? No foreplay?" I asked drily.

"Foreplay," he murmured, like this was a new idea.

And then he kissed me.

I wished I hadn't brought up foreplay. Eric was not a good kisser. Too wet, too deep, too much tongue, too too too. His hands were already in my shirt, like there was no point in easing me into the mood, like I was just some little high school senior with blue hair and a reputation for putting out.

I kept my eyes closed and thought of John. The way those

sleepy dark eyes would watch me as he put his hands down my shirt. The way he would take his time.

Honestly, it was no use. There was this whirling dervish in the way.

I pulled back from the kiss, but Eric followed me. I turned my head. He put his tongue in my ear. Finally I pressed one hand on his chest and held him off. "Give us a moment, won't you?" I said in a bad British accent, to lift the mood.

"What's the problem?" he growled, mouth still to my ear. "You want me to send you flowers now?"

Oh, yuck. "I just can't do this. I don't have the least desire to have sex with you when I'm not drunk."

His hands stopped in my shirt. Then started again. "Is tonight your last night with John? I'll call you tomorrow."

I couldn't believe this. I'd just told him I wasn't attracted to him when I was sober. He didn't care.

He had to know there was something going on with me and John—or there *had* been. I couldn't help but pronounce John's name with a dreamy drawl. Eric didn't care.

Eric probably had sex with Angie last night, and he didn't care about *that*, either.

I wouldn't have cared a week ago. But suddenly I did.

I gripped his wrists and tried to extract him from my shirt. "No, I don't think you should call me anymore."

He pressed me harder. I began to have a creepy feeling, full of fear. I'd expected him to pout, maybe, or tell me I was a stupid bitch. I hadn't expected him to keep insisting yes when I said no.

John's definition of a domestic flashed through my mind.

"Are you breaking up with me?" Eric hissed.

"I would, but I don't think I can," I said, keeping my voice even. "You need a relationship before you can break up."

We glared at each other. I could see him now in the cold dark. His eyes glittered and hardened. I had pushed until his control was gone, and there was nothing left but anger.

He was going to do something.

Feeling the pads of his fingers push into my flesh and my heartbeat pound in my ears, I tried to think through the fear. He was twice as big as me. Still. I didn't remember exactly what I'd done to Todd Pemberton when he tried to trap me in the elevator in the ninth grade, but it was legendary. Just let Eric try to trap me. Just let him try.

13

He pulled his hands out of my shirt and settled back on his side of the car.

"You shouldn't play games with me," he said snippily. "My dad knows every health inspector in the county. He could ruin Eggstra! Eggstra! like snapping his fingers."

That's when I really felt relieved. I'd thought he was going to hurt me. But if he was only going to be petty, I could handle that, easy.

"Eric," I said. "News flash. Your father does not give a shit about you. He does not give a shit whether you break up with your girlfriend. I've seen the way he looks at my hair. He'll be grateful my hair isn't associated with your family anymore."

"Hey. My father bailed me out of jail. Your father left you there to rot."

That stung, but I managed, "Your father didn't want to be further embarrassed. My parents are old hands at being embarrassed by me."

His jaw moved a little in the dim night, like he was chewing on something. He reached toward me, and I flinched back. But he was only reaching across me to pull a sandwich bag of pot out of the glove compartment.

"You were holding out on me," I said.

He fished a rolled joint and a lighter out of the loose weed. "Oh, shit. I forgot I lied to you. You want some? Maybe you'll change your mind about, you know. The other thing."

"No, and I don't particularly want to ride around with a policeman when I smell like pot smoke."

He flicked the lighter, touched the fire to the end of the joint, and took a long drag. Holding the smoke in his lungs, he suggested, "Roll down the window." He exhaled such a thick cloud that I could have caught a buzz off his breath.

I felt for the window controls before I thought. "They're automatic windows, Eric. Turn on the engine."

He moved to crank the car.

"No, wait!" I exclaimed. "What are you thinking? Why are you smoking pot before you take me back? You're not really going to drive. Stoned. To. The police station?"

"Why not? My dad can get me out of anything." He took another drag.

What could I do? I could leave the car and call John. Or just stand in the dark and wait for John to show up, since he loved the bridge so. But then I would have to explain how I got here, and why my motorcycle was at the police station.

And I would have saved myself while sending Eric off to have a wreck, killing innocent people. Not that there was any more chance of this now than all the other times he'd driven drunk and/or stoned, and I'd ridden with him. But I had to admit, seeing the dead woman last night had exactly the effect on me that John and the Powers That Be had intended. I hated it, but there it was.

Okay, I would call John and tell him to pull Eric over, then come retrieve me.

I got out and slammed the heavy door of the Beamer. Immediately hearing the low hum, I turned toward the bridge and looked for the train's headlight.

Blue lights burst to life behind me.

Heart racing, I whirled around and waited for John to say something to humiliate me through his megaphone.

"Driver, stay in the car. And don't even try to hide that contraband."

It was Officer Leroy's voice.

He left his engine humming as he walked from his cop car to the Beamer, coming close to me.

"I know what this looks like," I said quickly, before he could take out his handcuffs.

"Looks like every other time I catch kids parking." In the swirling blue light, I couldn't tell whether he was giving me the Disapproving Adult look.

"But it's not," I said. I racked my brain for any argument I could possibly make to convince him not to tell John. Even though I didn't care what John thought.

Officer Leroy nodded over his shoulder. "Go to After's car. He wants to talk to you."

After. I strained my eyes to see through the darkness. Sure enough, a second cop car was parked behind Officer Leroy's. Oh, no. "Can't *you* just give me the lecture?"

"He's pretty pissed," Officer Leroy said. "I wouldn't mess with him if I were you."

"*He's* pissed," I muttered. I was really mad. At least, I wanted to be really mad, and yet all I felt was scared and guilty. But there was nothing to feel scared or guilty about. I hadn't done anything wrong.

Well, maybe that was too strong a statement. I hadn't done anything *illegal.*

Shaking, I walked past Officer Leroy to John's car and pulled on the back door handle. It was locked. I slapped the door and heard the lock clunk open. Then I let myself into the backseat, crossed my legs primly, and hauled the door closed. I probably was locking myself in.

Through the metal grate, in the glow from the dashboard and Officer Leroy's headlights, John scribbled across forms on his clipboard. I watched the rearview mirror, waiting for the inevitable shock when our eyes met. And I tried to control my shaking so he wouldn't hear my movements against the vinyl seat in the warm car.

But he didn't meet my eyes in the rearview mirror. He turned all the way around to give me the look full-force through the metal grate.

Not outraged. Just hurt.

Which got me worse than anything else could have. Because it meant we could have salvaged 6:01 A.M. Thursday, and I had thrown it away.

Just to rub it in, a whiff of the cologne he'd worn for me tickled my nose.

"You know I check down here a lot." He'd never let me hear this tone from him before: hurt, accusatory, nineteen. "You wanted me to find you here, doing Eric."

"I wasn't *doing* Eric. I was standing outside the car when you got here, so that would be kind of a stretch."

"You intended to, though."

I wanted to turn away from the look, but his eyes held mine. My brain scrambled for a weapon to fight back with. "You followed me."

It worked. He actually sat back a little behind the grate, and went on the defensive. "I didn't follow you. I was headed into work a few minutes early to write my weekly report. I generally do it during my shift, but my shift's been more interesting than usual this week." He paused to watch my reaction.

My pulse quickened with that idiotic feeling again—he liked me! he liked me!—but I was very careful to show no reaction whatsoever.

He went on, "And then I recognized Eric's car, and I saw you turn in here."

I waited for him to hear himself. But of course he didn't. John was selectively daft. Finally I pointed out, "And then you *followed* me!"

He closed his eyes. "I—"

"I'm embarrassed enough already. Why'd you have to bring Leroy out here? You wanted me to feel as embarrassed as possible, right? You get off on making other people feel vulnerable and captured, because it makes *you* feel stronger and more in control."

"I—"

"This is what you want, right? This is exactly how you want me."

"No!" he shouted. His chest rose and fell rapidly. He put one hand up to grip the metal grate between us. His knuckles showed white. "If I had pulled Eric out of the car myself, I'm afraid of what I would have done to him."

He turned around in his seat and picked up his clipboard again. His hand shook on the pen.

I asked quietly, "Why are you pretending to write, when I already know you're just doing that to intimidate me?"

"Don't try to make me any angrier than I already am." He kept making notes and Xs and flipping through forms as he growled, "You're trying to get back at me for last night. You think I don't feel that, just because I'm wearing a uniform?"

I meant to keep acting sullen. But he was too mad. He demanded and maybe even deserved a real answer.

"You told me in the diner one night that I was feeling around for soft spots to stab you," I said. "What do you think you did to me last night? You've seen me faint before. You knew what would happen."

John shook his head. "I wasn't handcuffing you or locking you up. I had no idea you'd pass out. I just wanted to show you this accident to scare you, because I don't want you to get hurt." He turned around in his seat and pulled himself close to the metal grate between us, as if he would pull himself through it. "I care about you, Meg."

His sleepy dark eyes melted me. Almost. I wasn't falling for it. I glared at him. "You care about that dead girl."

"No, I care about *you*."

"Yeah, I understood that last night at the wreck. Nothing says *I love you* like a dead body."

He sighed through his nose. "You don't want to be tied down or held prisoner. Death is the ultimate prison, and you're headed there. That's what I'm trying to tell you."

"But you can't live your life worried about dying all the time. If you do, you're dead already. Like you."

He had completely forgotten to be big tough cop guy. He bit his lip gently and ran his fingers back through his short hair at the same time.

But we were tied. I'd crossed my arms on my chest.

"Even if you were mad at me," he said, "even if you thought I'd wronged you, I can't believe you would come here with Eric. It seems like the past week would have meant more to you."

"I didn't do him," I repeated.

"You were going to, though," he repeated.

Both these things seemed true, but didn't add up. "I wasn't going to," I said. "Maybe I thought I was, but I wasn't."

He watched me carefully. "Because of me?"

I sighed. "Because of you."

He gave me that dark, loving look. "Now is when I should hug you, and we would both feel so much better. But I can't in front of them." He nodded to Officer Leroy patting Eric down in the swirling blue light outside the car. Then he turned back to me and opened his hands in front of the metal grate. "Consider yourself hugged. Virtual hug."

I felt the virtual hug, warm and snug.

"All right," I said. "But from now on, every time you show me a dead body, I'm having sex with Eric."

"*God*, Meg!"

"That's as far as I can go for you right now."

We stared at each other through the grate for a few moments. Though his stern expression didn't change, he did cock his head, as if looking at me from a new angle might help.

Finally he turned around in his seat and faced the steering wheel. Like nothing had happened—no induced fainting, no near-sex with pot-smoking boyfriend, no virtual hug—he said, "Come up in the front seat where you belong, and let's get out of here. We have work to do."

WE DROVE TO THE INTERSTATE AND downtown and the bridge and McDonald's and Martini's and Eggstra! Eggstra! and the bridge and the bad side of town and the Birmingham Junction and the bridge. Then Lois radioed to us about an attempted break-in at one of the smaller stores near Target in the town's main shopping center, which some of our more unsophisticated citizens, including my mom, referred to as a *mall*.

Lois said the suspects were driving an old Aztek. We cruised all the way around the shopping center parking lot and behind the buildings. No Aztek. As usual, the crime was over by the time John got there.

He parked the cop car, and we walked under the shopping center awning. He checked the doors of all the stores and shone his flashlight through the windows to make sure. Speakers under the awning played the Birmingham radio station as if it were daytime shopping hours, not 4 A.M.

As if John and I were on a shopping date.

He tried the locked door of Dixie Dental and played his flashlight beam around the waiting room. Offhandedly he said, "We haven't talked about anything important the whole shift."

"Like?" I hoped he meant we should talk about 6:01 A.M. Thursday, which was approximately two hours from now. I hoped we were back on.

"Like cancer," he said.

Now *there* was a disappointment. But I could tell this was really bothering him. He avoided my eyes and kept examining Dixie Dental's posters of smiling cartoon tooth people, to make it easier for me to answer.

"I wouldn't have pushed you so hard if I'd known," he said.

"Don't ask me how I went to high school with you and never heard about it."

I followed him as he walked up to Bama Blinds, Curtains, and More, which strangely did not have window coverings. He tried that door. I focused on where I was walking. Despite looking down, or maybe because of it, I tripped over my own feet and nearly fell trying to avoid a crack. I didn't want to break my mother's back. In fact, of all the things I regretted about the way I handled leukemia (or failed miserably to do so), I was most sorry for worrying my mother. Every time my dad guilted me about her, I just wanted even more to escape, which got me in more trouble. I wished I could take it all back.

Lord knew how many times I'd broken my mother's back already. And the walkway awning seemed awfully low all of a sudden. I stepped off the sidewalk and into the empty parking lot, where it was safer. Tall light poles held up the dark blue starless sky.

"The treatment dragged on until I was a sophomore," I said. "But all the business of my hair falling out, the ambulance rushing to school to pick me up when I collapsed in the hall, everything that would get your attention—that was in eighth grade, middle school, when you were already in ninth grade at the high school. There's no reason you would have heard about it. And it doesn't even make sense for me to get on you about your cigarettes. I didn't get cancer by smoking cigarettes. I got it because I'm lucky. I guess I just don't want anyone else to go through that."

Especially not you. I thought it, but I couldn't say it.

He turned on the sidewalk and faced me, looking down at me below him in the parking lot. "Tell me what happened," he coaxed.

"Oh, no. It's not a big deal. I know I act like it is, but . . ."

The sickeningly inspirational Phil Collins song came through the speakers. I couldn't help smiling.

"Okay, I'll tell you, because this is my theme song. 'Look Through My Ass.'"

John showed me his dimples. "I think it's 'Look Through My Eyes.'"

"No, no, no. See, I had an adverse reaction to the chemotherapy. They kept switching me to different drugs and starting over. I was on my deathbed for months. In fact, the ambulance Tiffany's riding around in now was my deathbed."

Nodding to show me he was still listening, he turned away and shone his flashlight into the store again so I could talk, which I appreciated. As he finished examining Bama Blinds, Curtains, and More and moved up the sidewalk to the next store, he half turned to make sure I followed along with him in the parking lot.

I explained over the music, "I had to get all these MRIs so they could keep track of my multiple organ failure. I don't know if you've ever had an MRI, but they slide you headfirst into this excruciatingly small tube. I would always close my eyes and sing this song at the top of my lungs to the creepy radiologist looking at pictures of the inside of my body. I swear, it's this sweet song from a Disney movie they showed in the rec room on the pediatric ward, and it's got the highfalutin full-blown orchestra and the violins and everything, and then there's Phil Collins singing, 'Look through my aaaaaaaaaass.'"

John's shoulders shook with laughter. He actually lowered his flashlight, closed his eyes, and let himself do nothing but laugh for a few seconds.

And I glowed, just from making John laugh.

I was such an idiot.

He let out one last small laugh and continued up the sidewalk. "That's where your claustrophobia came from," he called over his shoulder.

"No."

14

What happened was, I was running every day in PE, and I started to feel really tired. That's how they found out I had leukemia. They told me I needed treatment that would make me feel a lot worse than the disease. I told them where to go. My mom got mad and said I was vain and I didn't want my hair to fall out. Well, yeah, that was an issue. But the problem was more that I didn't feel like I was dying. I *knew* I was dying because they told me, but I didn't *feel* like I was dying. I just felt tired. And if I took chemo, I'd feel like I was dying. The doctor's eyes rolled back in his head, and he called in the hospital's child psychologist to convince me.

She wanted me to post to the supportive cancer blog online and sign up for summer cancer camp. Cancer can be fun! I told her what I thought of cancer camp. That's when I dyed my hair pink, before one of the psych appointments. It hasn't been my natural color since. Just my little way of saying *screw you*. Not that I had anything against this poor lady. She was doing her job. But I didn't want to be counseled. I wanted not to be dying. They switched me to a different psychologist, a man who used tough love, to no avail. I'd lived through thirteen years of tough love from my dad. I told Mr. Psychologist where he could put his tough love.

The first treatment day came and went. I refused to do it. They waited a few days and counseled me some more and wheedled and pleaded and almost had me convinced, but I backed out at the last minute. By that time my mom was all cried out, always sitting in a comfy chair and crocheting oceans of blue afghan like it would cushion her from reality, and my dad was fed up. He told me I was killing my mother. He said we would go to this third chemo appointment and I would let them put the IV in my arm and I would smile while they did it or there would be no more iPod, no more TV, no more friends, no more meeting boys at the movies, grounded for life. Fine. We got to the hospital in Birmingham a little early. I asked my parents if we could drive to Dreamland and grab some barbecue to go for my last meal before I started taking chemo and barfing. I asked nicely. They said sure. My dad left me and my mom in the car while he went in. I asked my mom if I could have a sweet tea with my barbecue. She said sure and went inside after my dad.

I bailed out of the car and took off running up Thirteenth Avenue, running for my life. I ran until I couldn't run anymore. I didn't get far. Birmingham is uphill both ways and, oh yeah, I had leukemia. I made it past ten houses and around a bend in the road before I collapsed in somebody's azaleas. It was about this time of year, chilly but everything was blooming. A cherry tree scattered delicate pink petals across me as I lay there. That's when I finally realized I was going to die. And what was I being so emo about? People died every day. I was nothing special. On the other hand, most girls my age, like Tiffany and Julie Meadows and LaShonda Smith, were sitting in algebra class at that very moment, humming pop songs and memorizing the Pythagorean theorem while I was expiring in a stranger's shrubbery. Why me? I had been just like them until a few weeks before. But I wasn't one of them anymore. Now I was a teenager who defied her parents and cussed at adults. Dying made more sense now that I deserved it.

A cop car came around the corner. I knew instantly my dad had called the heat on me. I tried to stand up and run, but I was still out of breath. They tackled me and handcuffed me and I struggled and cussed, beyond caring. They drove a few blocks and parked at the emergency room of the hospital. They tried to get me out of the car and I started kicking. They strapped my legs together and picked me up like a sheep going to slaughter. My dad pulled in right behind them. My mom was crying in the passenger seat. I could hear her, even with all the noise of the city I could hear her crying inside the car, and my dad told her to *go park the fucking car* and he followed us inside. The two cops carried me into the elevator with my dad. Somebody got on the elevator with us, some hapless secretary who had nothing to do with us, somebody you would normally nod to politely when she got on the elevator.

Suddenly it struck me as hilarious that I would have this thought about propriety while hanging facedown from two policemen with my hands and feet bound. I giggled. The policemen asked if I could be a good girl and go nicely to my execution now. I started kicking again as best I could, bucking. For the first time in this whole ordeal, I wanted to hurt someone.

We got off on our floor. The cops put me on a stretcher, but they stayed to help hold me while they wheeled me down the hall. All the kids on the ward stopped short in their doorways, wearing their bright pajamas, and watched me pass by cussing. Nurses clumped around us and traveled down the hall with us, shielding the innocents from me. They whispered *resistant* and *uncooperative* and *noncompliant*, which are hospital terms for *hysterical brat in room 86*. I screamed anything I could think of to make them let me go. *I don't really have cancer. My parents want to kill me. My dad is trying to get rid of me.* The nurses hissed anything they could think of to shut me up. *You're acting like a three-year-old. You're scaring the other children. We had an autistic kid in here last week who screamed less than you.* Trailing after us, the doctor spoke with an Indian accent and a British clip on his words, so different from my dad's southern drawl, it was like they weren't even speaking the same language.

Doctor: She's the borderline age where we'd respect her wishes and counsel her longer, seeking her consent to treatment.

Dad: I know.

Doctor: It's also the borderline time when if we don't treat her, she'll be at high risk of treatment failure no matter what we do later.

Dad: I know.

Doctor: But her chart suggests she is likely to remain combative—

Dad: Look, Doc, I know. Just strap her down and give it to her.

We got to the room and the cops pressed me down on the bed until the nurses could get the tethers around my wrists and ankles. I strained against the bindings until my hands went numb. This wasn't happening, this couldn't possibly be the way it ended, but it was. I screamed so loud, I could hardly hear the nurse telling my dad he would need to fill out a form to consent to them restraining me and a form to consent to them sedating me, and maybe he would like to come to the nurse's station to do that. He left the room. Another nurse whispered calmly in my ear, *Sweetie-pie, which hand do you want the IV in?* She tried to fool me into thinking I had some choice as she gave me a shot of tranquilizer. *Calm down, sweetie-pie, it'll all be over soon.* I felt it right away. They took the restraints off. I thought, *I'm free now*, but I couldn't move. It was like the restraints were still there. I went to sleep, and later I woke up dying.

I went willingly to every chemo session after that, and every radiation session, because I didn't want to be strapped down again. Sometimes my hair would grow back in a sad little way between sessions, and my mom would tell me how pretty I looked, and I would dye my hair purple. And every time I had an adverse reaction and started to die again, I would turn to my dad and say, *I told you so.*

JOHN AND I WERE SITTING ON the hood of the police car. Actually John was leaning back against the hood with one boot on the pavement and one boot cocked behind him on the bumper. I balanced on the hood, curled into a ball with my knees to my chest, rubbing the back of my left hand where the IV had been. Now that I had blinked back to the present, I kept blinking to stop myself from crying. I did not cry.

John watched me, dark eyes inscrutable. His shoulders rose as he inhaled through his nose. He was about to say something like *I am so sorry* or *I had no idea* or even *You are a terrible person.* In which case I was going to lose it. There was a reason I did not talk about this.

He said, "I feel sorry for the officers on *that* call."

I laughed and laughed and laughed. This was a good excuse to cry just a little. I kept laughing and wiped the tears from my eyes. "Historically the fuzz loves to see me coming."

He laughed, too, and put one hand up to his eyes. But he looked down and away, and I looked down and away, so I could tell myself his tears were my imagination.

He sniffed. Because he'd turned away, his voice sounded muffled as he said, "Your dad loves you, and he was scared."

I leaned forward and took John's hand in both of mine. "John, this week, I know you've tried to show me I'm living on the edge and I'm not immortal. I get it. But I've had cancer, and nothing will ever seem dangerous to me after that. So I would appreciate it if you would just fucking quit." I patted his hand in a friendly way that turned into more of a slap before I let him go. "Anyway, it's over now."

He gazed down at his abused hand. "Is it?"

"Well, sure. It was worse than your garden-variety childhood leukemia because I was pretty old when I got it. It could come back. But probably not."

"I mean, it's not over in your mind. You're still on that table, strapped down, with an IV in your hand."

Watching the gold police badge glint as his chest rose and fell, I stroked my fingers down a lock of my hair. It surprised me, how long it had gotten. When I flipped it in front of my eyes to examine it, I was surprised again that it was blue.

"So, what happened after that in the hospital?" John asked. "You came to terms with it."

"I wouldn't go *that* far."

"You became a role model for the ward."

"Uh, no."

"But the other kids hung out in your room."

I looked up at him. "Yes! It was like Grand Central freaking Station in there. How'd you know?"

"And you survived."

"Yeah, and some other kids there didn't. My roommate died."

177

As soon as I said it, I wished I hadn't. I'd stepped off the path I walked down every day and put one foot in crap. I had no intention of ruining my magical last night of incarceration with John remembering Lizzie Dark, who was ten years old, whose parents brought her golden retriever to visit her on the ward every Sunday afternoon, and who always beat me at gin.

God, Lizzie. I teetered on the cusp of crying for real. It hurt too much to hold it in.

"Meg," John said beside me. I turned to face more grilling from him. I knew why I was claustrophobic, all right. But knowing why didn't make it go away. I wondered what it would be like to see the dark blue sky above us not as heavy drapes of cloth, the top of a circus tent, but as an infinite expanse. As everybody else saw it.

John had more important things to worry about than my neuroses. Listening to Lois on the radio at his shoulder, he said, "The panic button was set off at the Shop Till You Drop. I'll bet that's our Aztek."

He was right. "Here you are," John told the Aztek, which was parked at the Shop Till You Drop convenience store. On the shoulder across the highway from the store, he coasted the cop car to a stop with the headlights off and cut the engine.

It wasn't often that we sat in the car without the radio. Or the heat. The cold silence closed in around us.

My body went even colder as I watched what was going on inside the convenience store. One man pointed a rifle at someone down behind the counter, where we couldn't see. A second man with a rifle stood in front of the counter, with his back to the plate glass windows. A third man over in the groceries propped his rifle against a shelf so he could open a pack of something I couldn't quite make out from this distance. Maybe Oreos.

John stared at the store, hardly blinking. He gripped the steering wheel with both hands. I could feel his tension in the air.

"You're waiting for backup, I guess." I hoped.

He nodded once, without taking his eyes from the store.

"Why are they conducting this crime in front of the window, where anyone could see them?" I asked, just to get him talking. To release some of his tension. Or mine. "I realize it's four thirty in the morning, but you never know when a cop is sitting across the highway, watching you."

He huffed a little laugh through his nose. "Same reason they're making the clerk open the safe under the counter, rather than taking the money from the cash register and running. They know the longer they stay, the more likely they are to get caught. But they're high. Poor judgment. Same reason they're riding around town committing crimes in an Aztek." He took a deep breath, let it out slowly, and lowered his voice almost to a whisper. "When I go in, be sure to duck down."

My heart thumped uncomfortably in my chest. I wanted to ask, *You mean they're really going to use those guns?* I wasn't sure I'd ever seen a genuine gun in person, except John's. I had thought he'd been in danger previous nights, but it had all been distant and unreal until now.

What I ended up asking was, "Doesn't this car have bulletproof glass?" I leaned forward a little so I could see his face better.

Then wished I hadn't. The worry lines had appeared between his brows. "More like bullet-resistant."

I sat back in my seat and watched the men inside the store. Where *was* John's backup? If I sat here waiting much longer, I would panic. And I couldn't hear John breathing. It was so quiet in the car, my ears rang.

"Are you scared?" I whispered.

"I'm well trained."

Yes, he was well trained to enter a robbery in progress with three guns pointed at him. Or well trained to hide that he was scared.

His death-hold on the steering wheel gave him away.

"Do you want me to kiss you for luck?" I asked.

His eyes cut to me for a split second, then returned to the store. He waited so long that I thought he wasn't going to answer. He would ignore my inappropriate question.

Then he said, "Yes."

I scooted next to him on the seat. The heat of his leg soaked through my jeans. Inhaling his cologne, I leaned my head toward his. He didn't turn to me or take his eyes off the store—and of course I didn't want him to, because that would not be safe.

I closed my eyes and softly, slowly kissed his jaw.

His big hand closed over my knee, then slid up my leg. His fingers massaged as they went.

I opened my eyes again to make sure I wasn't ruining his

official police work. He still watched the store. But when I ended the kiss, he sighed.

I kissed him again, farther back toward his ear. He took a sharp breath. His hand clamped my thigh.

Reluctantly, I pulled back. Sliding my leg out from under his hand, I scooted over to the passenger seat. I was liable to get him in trouble. And strangely, even though he *still* stared at the store, I felt like I had more self-control than he did right then.

His hand crept into my lap, found my hand, and pulled it to the middle of the seat.

We were holding hands.

Officer After was holding hands in his police vehicle with a known criminal with blue hair. He must have had a premonition he was going to die.

A low hum vibrated the car. I turned around. A cop car parked close behind ours, headlights off. Two more parked behind that.

John gave my hand a final squeeze. Then, looking away from me, he left the car with a musical clanking of equipment on his belt and closed the door softly.

He had a brief powwow at the front bumper with the other cops. The four of them crossed the highway together in that way cops had of moving, casually and calmly, with frightening purpose. They walked quickly toward the store, but off to the side, where they couldn't be seen through the front windows. When they reached the building, Officer Leroy and another cop crouched at the front corner. John and a fourth cop disappeared around the back.

The men inside the store went on as if nothing were about

to happen. One had finally gotten the contents of the safe from the clerk and was stuffing his coat pockets with stacks of bills. Another still stood guard very ineffectively, with his back to the cop cars across the highway. The other ate Oreos.

Officer Leroy spoke into the radio on his shoulder and pointed his gun up in the air, ready.

Inside the store, a door behind the counter burst open. John stood in the doorway with his pistol extended. The suspect on guard raised his rifle at John.

Then lowered his rifle. All of them dropped their rifles and put their hands up as John advanced into the room, pointing his pistol at one suspect and then another.

The other three cops swarmed in. I couldn't hear them of course, but they all turned very red in the face and looked to be screaming their heads off. They directed the suspects to kick their rifles away, lie down on the floor, put their hands behind their backs.

John still covered his fellow officers, protecting them, switching the aim of his pistol from one suspect to another. Finally, when all the suspects were cuffed and the cops stepped back, John relaxed his arms and holstered his weapon.

Then he looked up at me. I was sure he couldn't see me watching him at that distance, out in the dark. But he looked up at me. And gave me a little wave.

I gasped in the freezing car, and realized I'd been holding my breath. I was *so relieved*.

And not. Because at some time in the last five days, I had freaking fallen in love with John After.

15

We pulled up at the jail/courthouse/city hall, and he turned off the engine. He didn't make a move to get out. Neither did I.

"Is it 6:01 A.M. Thursday?" I was wearing my watch, but I was more interested in what time *he* had.

He glanced at his watch. "It's 6:05."

"Did we miss it?"

He laughed.

"So where do we . . ." I looked around the car, then at him. "You don't want to, do you."

He turned his dark eyes on me. It wasn't the look of love. It wasn't the hard, angry look, either. Damn it, I couldn't read the look.

I *knew* not to get too close, because it was easier to see what was going on from the outside. I knew this, and I'd gotten too close anyway. I shouldn't have told him what happened four years ago. He thought I was diseased. He knew I was evil. Now I was about to get hurt.

I breathed, "You were alone, on night shift, with a girl, and you were bored."

"Why would I have taken you seriously?" he protested. "You told me you don't plan. I thought *you* were bored. You'd get in trouble if you didn't show up for work at the diner now, anyway."

He had a point. The diner hadn't occurred to me. That was one problem with not planning. You got in trouble a lot.

"Right." I leaned down and grabbed my notebook from the floor. "Pop the trunk, would you?"

I didn't even slam my door. I managed to close it properly. When he didn't open the trunk right away, I knocked on it politely. It opened. I retrieved my motorcycle helmet, closed the trunk gently, and walked over to slip the notebook into the bag on my motorcycle.

John opened his window and called to me. "You know you're not off the hook until you send the DA your project proposal and tell her what you've learned."

"I e-mailed it to her yesterday from work." I got on my bike.

He leaned a little farther out the window. "You're still not going to give me a hint what it's about?"

"Yeah, John. Here's what I learned by wasting my spring break with the police. I learned that you're a fucking asshole." I started the engine so I wouldn't hear anything else he said, then put on my helmet. Briefly I considered taking off my helmet, hooking it to my bike, and roaring away. But that would just make him come after me. I didn't want him to come after me. Repeat: I did not want him to come after me. And anyway, I couldn't afford another traffic ticket.

I fastened my helmet and *then* roared away, without looking back.

As if I had the last laugh. The last laugh was definitely his. He had done what he set out to do. He had taught the dead girl a lesson.

IT FELT LIKE THE LONGEST SHIFT of my greasy spoon career.

Some days I almost enjoyed parts of working at Eggstra! Eggstra! Cooking. Making up new recipes. Observing the more colorful customers, like the hunters and fishermen out-boasting one another, or the cheating-heart couples using the diner as the starting point for their rendezvous. If given a choice, they always picked the Princess Diana table, like she gave cheating a good name.

Today I didn't enjoy it. I botched orders and burned my finger on the grill. I couldn't concentrate on work with the last five days playing over and over in my mind. Screaming at John outside his car at the bridge. Touching him in his apartment. Kissing him in his car. Watching him walk calmly to his imminent death in the convenience store, while I stayed behind like his worried missus, whipping up a fruit cobbler for him in my mind.

I felt more of a connection with him than I'd ever felt with anyone in my life. Was it possible I had *imagined* this vibe? Maybe so, I decided as I wiped our table carefully and turned the busts of Elvis toward the wall.

The other days this week, I'd taken a break mid-morning. I'd left Corey in charge of the front and checked my e-mail in the office. Today we were so busy, I didn't get a break until almost two in the afternoon, quitting time. Good news, though. The DA had accepted my bullshit proposal to discourage other errant teens from following in my footsteps. In fact, the city was instituting my proposal today. Suddenly I was a model citizen. Go figure.

John would love my project. Or hate it. And me. Not that I cared anymore.

I switched off the computer and sauntered back into the diner to wait out the few minutes left in my shift by scrubbing chair legs or something else the paid employees didn't bother to do, and— oh, yeah—obsessing about John some more. Would you believe it, a customer had the audacity to walk in just then. I couldn't see his face in the blinding beam of sunlight behind him. But I could tell from the way he walked he was a teenager.

On my way toward him, I grabbed a menu from the stack. I wished I could tell this kid to go to McDonald's, because teenagers didn't tip. But he might cause a hullabaloo that would get back to my parents. I knew this from experience.

When I walked in front of him, where his head and shoulders blocked the sun, I stopped dead. It was John. The sun behind his back made the edges of his blond hair glow like a halo.

I had never seen him look so good. I mean, Officer After was manly. Johnafter the runner was hot. But this boy wore loose jeans and a faded T-shirt that clung to his chest. An Incubus T-shirt, the one with a heart inside a grenade. His hair was short, but not abnormally so. It stuck out in strange places like he'd run his hands through it on the drive over here. Despite the halo, he was a mess.

Exactly as a boy should be.

I looked around for Corey. He could wait on John instead of me. But he must have taken a bathroom break. Then I glanced out the front windows into the parking lot, on the chance Bonita had pulled up. Usually she was fifteen minutes early for her shift, which was miraculous considering what my parents paid people. No such luck today.

John walked right past me. He slid into our booth, the Elvis table.

I walked toward him and stopped in front of the table, holding the menu awkwardly. At a complete loss for words. For once.

"I don't need a menu," he said.

I was not supposed to be flabbergasted at seeing him. And definitely not ecstatic. I was supposed to be angry with him for blowing me off this morning. I called up some fake anger. "What do *you* want?"

"The Meg Special." He pinned me to the spot with his dark, sleepy eyes and looked me up and down.

That did make me angry. "We're all out."

"Then why are you still advertising?"

Two could play that game. I slid the menu in front of him

and put both hands on the table. Leaning forward so he could see down my shirt, I said low, "I did the crime. I did the time. You got nothing on me, copper."

I started to stand up straight, but he covered my hand with his hand and gestured with his eyes to the booth seat beside him. "Sit down."

What he'd told me at Martini's flashed through my mind: *You want to be higher than the suspects, talking down to them.* Right now, I was talking down to him. If I sat, *he'd* be talking down to *me*.

He raised his eyebrows and smiled. Both dimples showed.

I sat down.

He squeezed my hand and leaned closer. I felt the warmth of his body and caught the scent of his cologne. "I want to show you something," he said.

"Thanks, but you've shown me plenty." I tried to back out of the booth.

He held me in place with his hand on mine. "No, nothing like that. Something different. Something good."

So John finally wanted to show me something good, huh? I let my eyes travel from his strong neck down to the T-shirt covering his broad chest. I could think of several sights that would qualify. "Like what?"

"The beach."

Fighting the sudden urge to cry, I pulled my hand out from under his and sat back. I pointed at him, as he'd pointed at me with his pen in the cop car one night. "Don't tease me."

"Miami's too far, though. I have to work tomorrow night. I was hoping you'd settle for the Redneck Riviera."

Of course I would settle for the Florida Panhandle. With John. And of course he couldn't be serious.

And of course I couldn't go, anyway. "I have to be back before you do, for my shift at six A.M. tomorrow. And don't tell me you forgot about the diner. You were kind enough to remind me this morning."

"No, I haven't forgotten. I figure it will take us five hours to drive down there—"

"Three, if you let me drive."

He cleared his throat and gave me a stern look. "It will take *me* five hours to drive down there and five to drive back. That leaves you six hours of spring break."

I was beginning to think he was serious. "When will I sleep? I have to sleep before work tomorrow."

"You can sleep in my truck on the way down, and on the way back."

"When will *you* sleep?"

"I've been asleep for the last seven hours, and I'll sleep again when you go to work tomorrow morning." He leaned back in the booth and tapped his fingers on the menu. "Next argument."

I hadn't slept since yesterday, right after my run and my conversation with Tiffany about the possibility of her becoming a slut-whore. And right before I almost slut-whored myself to Eric again. It seemed like a year ago, but nothing in the diner had changed. Same bright afternoon sunlight slanting through the front windows. Same secondhand tables, same kitschy saltshakers.

The only remarkable thing was John, still drop-dead gorgeous and hunky, but in a teenager's clothes.

Officer After, transformed into a boyfriend.

"Why the sudden change of heart?" I asked.

He took my hand again and whispered, "No sudden change of heart."

"You mean, this morning, you already intended to invite me to the beach?"

He nodded.

I pulled my hand away and whacked him on the chest. "Then why'd you act like you hated me?"

He grinned. "You've said you don't plan. I didn't want you to stand me up."

"You mean you were *manipulating* me?"

He touched my bottom lip with one finger. "Just say yes."

I lost myself in his dark eyes. "Yes."

Bonita had come in by then. I asked her to serve John steak and eggs with steamed vegetables while I ran to the trailer and took the quickest shower of my greasy spoon career. Suddenly my career had sped up, with my pulse.

I pulled on clean jeans and the skimpiest shirt I owned, which was saying a lot because I owned some fine examples. As I saw it, the occasion called for cleave and even belly button. I paused for a split second in front of the mirror and wished for the umpteenth time this week that my hair wasn't blue, but I was already on my way out the door.

"I KNOW WHAT YOU'RE THINKING, AND I want you to plan for once," John called over the noise of the surf. "It's going to be a long ride back in wet underwear."

Uncanny, how he'd known I was thinking of plunging my whole body into the water, clothes and all. The cold night back home had lifted for the warmest day of the year so far. Florida was even warmer. And even though the ocean was still cool, I longed to experience it in every way I could, for the short time it was mine.

But John was right, as usual, damn him. "You keep your mind off my underwear," I said. Actually, I was delighted to have him think about my underwear.

My face must have given me away, because he took my hand.

We sloshed together through the waves, with our jeans rolled up past our knees. When we'd first gotten here half an hour before, the sun was still up over the dark blue ocean. I had heard the Gulf Coast had the world's whitest beaches, but I hadn't expected them to be this white. They weren't paper-white, but just off—the color of John's hands.

Now the beach was tinted pink, the clouds and ocean glowed neon pink, and a huge orange sun sank in the violet sky. Every time I glanced at John, I expected to look back at the sunset and discover it had been a figment of my imagination. Of course, every time I glanced at the sunset, I expected to look back at John and find he'd disappeared.

He swung my hand as we splashed along. "It's so beautiful that I wouldn't know how to begin to draw it."

"You've drawn the Matterhorn, John. I'm sure you'd manage a Florida sunset."

"This one is special. It would be hard to convey how jarring and in-your-face it is." He turned to me. "And still so beautiful."

I smiled back at him, choosing to tune out the *jarring* part and listen to the *beautiful* part. "Besides, where would you put the elephants wearing hats?"

"I think I put those in because I'm not confident in my art. Other people aren't as likely to judge me if I already have elephants wearing hats in the drawing, judging it themselves."

"You know what might help that problem?"

The light had faded to the point that I couldn't make out his hard, dark eyes. I was glad. "A college education in art?" he asked flatly.

"No. Drawing nothing but the bridge over and over. There are no judgmental creatures in your drawing of the railroad bridge."

We walked on in our silence underneath the roar of the ocean. I waited for him to get revenge.

Here it came. "Something's been bothering me since I found out you had leukemia. Your parents stuck with you through it. Doesn't that make you feel like you owe them?"

"They're my parents. What else could they do? Let me die in the street?"

Strangely, we were still holding hands as we threw sharp darts at each other. But he stopped playfully swinging my hand.

"Of course I owe them," I said. "Insurance didn't cover everything. That's why they make me work at the diner for free. My dad says I'm still paying off the methotrexate and daunomycin."

I could feel John shaking his head above me, like I was missing the point. "You needed them, and they helped you. Now they need you. Don't you want to stay and help them? Don't you feel grateful?"

"I feel grateful. Grateful, like, send them a card. Grateful, like, build myself a career and make them proud of me. Grateful, like, have children someday and bring them back to town for Christmas. Not grateful, like, spend the rest of my life with them, running their shitty little diner in the middle of nowhere."

I wished he hadn't brought it up. Or I hadn't. We had to get off this subject and stay off it for the rest of the night, or we'd never get laid.

He must have had the same idea, because he dropped my hand, pinched my ass, and dashed away as best he could through the knee-deep water.

I slogged after him. We played grab-ass in the fading light. Which morphed into a hundred-yard dash up and down the gray beach. He won every time. So I craftily morphed it into a touch football game with a balled-up towel. What we played didn't matter so long as his big hands grazed my waist every few minutes, fueling the fire. I felt like I'd never been terminally ill.

At some point we got hungry and walked toward the road to a stand that sold fried seafood. This place made Eggstra! Eggstra! look like fine dining. But when we took the boxes back down to the moonlit beach and set out our picnic on our towels, I made a startling discovery. The shrimp were fresh. Someone had caught them off the coast that very afternoon. The shrimp we served at Eggstra! Eggstra! had been frozen for God knew how many decades. In fact, I probably had never eaten fresh shrimp before in my life. But I recognized them when I tasted them.

I began to have the sneaking suspicion this night was too good to be true.

I *knew* it was too good to be true when it got even better. John pulled out his cell phone and called Will. "I'm down for just a few hours, and I want to show the lady a good time while we're here," he shouted over the roar of the tide. "Where's the party?"

He had me pegged. I loved parties.

He laughed into the phone. "No, the lady would not happen to have blue hair. Her hair is indigo. Cyan."

"Violet," I mouthed.

He reached behind my head and ran his fingers down the purple strands in back. He stroked absently while he finished talking on the phone, as if setting my blood on fire were the most natural thing in the world.

16

We drove the truck a few miles down the beach highway to an enormous nightclub on stilts. The music from inside pulsed so loudly that the sand strewn across the road vibrated with every beat. We paid cover at the door and walked all the way through the building to get where we were going.

John held my hand like a vise so we didn't get separated among the writhing bodies. I watched the looks on girls' faces as we passed. They checked John out for long seconds. Then they saw we were holding hands. Then they checked me out: hair, face, boobs, belly button, boobs, face, ending with a long and pointed look at my hair. Then another glance at John, like, *When you get tired of this, call me.* All the mascara, cleave, and midriff in the world didn't make up for the fact that I had blue hair and blue hair was weird. I definitely didn't want to get in a fight with a girl in my six hours at the beach, but I did try to step on their toes in their high-heeled sandals as I passed.

In back of the club, we had the best of both worlds: our white beach and black ocean and white moon, plus a throbbing party. Hundreds of college kids danced inside a square of tiki torches. We kicked off our shoes and crossed the sand.

Alone at the edge of the crowd, in a bank of plastic chairs that the rising tide threatened to sweep away, Will nursed a beer. We recognized the silhouette of his curly hair against the sky. Now that John wasn't in uniform, he and Will gave each other a big boy-hug, swatting each other hard on the back. Will turned to me and moved to hug me. Then he saw John's look and folded his arms around his beer cup.

John leaned in. "I'm going to get her a drink. Don't steal her while I'm gone."

"Are you crazy?" Will asked. "I wouldn't dare steal from the *police academy*."

John turned to me. "Frozen daiquiri?"

"Piña colada, please."

"Virgin?" He wasn't asking my permission. He was just making sure I knew he wasn't going to try to swipe me any alcohol.

"That's optimistic," I said.

He frowned at me and glared at Will before heading across the beach toward one of the bars in thatched huts. Apparently I was not allowed to make sex jokes in front of Will. Surely John wasn't *still* jealous.

"Speaking of virgins," I said to Will.

He eyed me warily. "Pardon?" He sipped his beer.

"Spring break's almost over. You're here alone. Time's a-wastin'."

"Wha—" he spluttered into his cup. "Am I giving out *virgin vibes?*"

"Kind of."

He gaped at me, then closed his mouth and shook his head in disgust. "I wanted to come here. At least, I thought I did. I really like to look. But when it comes right down to it . . . I want it to mean something, you know?"

I nodded. "Actually, no, but I can imagine."

A cell phone rang. "And don't you dare tell John I said that," Will went on. "Some things guys just don't say to each other." He pulled his phone from his back pocket and looked at the screen. "Speak of the Devil." He clicked the phone on. "Yes, Governor?" Then he whirled around, glancing in every direction around the beach. "You're *watching* us? Where are you?"

"He's sneaky," I said.

Will clicked the phone off and pocketed it. "John told me to move six inches to the left." He picked up his plastic chair and edged away from me in the wet sand. "He really likes you."

"He does stuff that makes me think so," I admitted. "Bringing me to the beach."

"That's serious," Will agreed.

"And then he does stuff that makes me think he doesn't like me at all. For instance, Tuesday night, he made sure I saw a dead body in a car wreck. That's not my idea of date night."

Will cringed, and shook his shoulders like he had the shivers. "He takes that cop stuff very seriously. But I know he likes you, Meg. The night I saw y'all at McDonald's, he called me from Martini's and told me to back off. *You* didn't think I was coming on to you, did you?"

"No."

"Neither did I." Will was a little drunk, I saw.

"Wait a minute," I said. It was my turn to gape at Will. "He called you from Martini's? He was supposed to be breaking up a bar fight! I feared for his safety! Bastard."

"Yeah, I think the fight was over. He just talked to the manager for a second. Then he probably stood in the corner and glowered at people like he does, and called me, pretending it was Official Police Business." He imitated John in a low, serious voice. "'I'm in charge of her while I'm at work, and I can't have my best friend hitting on her.'"

"Will, that sounds like he *doesn't* like me."

"He likes you, trust me. He doesn't *want* to like you."

"Why not?"

"Because you're leaving. And he's staying. That's exactly the problem he got into with Angie." He traced a heart in the condensation on his cup. "Personally, I didn't see why they couldn't stay together. Birmingham is only a twenty-minute drive from town. It would have been hard for them to see each other because of John's weird working and sleeping schedule, but they could have done it. It hardly even qualifies as a long-distance relationship. I think John just wasn't that into her." He rolled his eyes. "There's not a whole lot there, anyway."

"*She* broke up with *him*, though."

"Right," Will said, pointing at me. "But now she's interested in him again."

"It makes perfect sense to me that she'd be conflicted, if she *has* any sense. He's this awesomely handsome, really cool guy who's chained himself to a bridge. He's hot, he's cold." I moved toward Will, and I didn't care whether John was watching or not. This was important. "When you were a kid, did you ever watch *The X-Files?* Mulder is this smart, cute, funny guy who's obsessed with catching the aliens who stole his sister. He's totally oblivious to the red-haired Scully standing right in front of him—"

"I don't think John is totally oblivious to you. I don't think that's possible. You talk really loudly."

"—and if he happens to throw her a kiss, she'll take it. If he happens to think to screw her, she'll *really* take it. And she says things to him like, 'Logically, Mulder, this doesn't make sense, please let go,' and she pats him on the shoulder and hopes he'll screw her again."

Will was staring at me with big eyes. I'd forgotten he was a virgin. Talking to him about sex was like talking to Tiffany.

"Well, I'm not Scully," I went on. "I can't pat John and comfort him. I want to put my hands around his neck and shake him and scream, 'What are you doing?'" I demonstrated in the empty air and I hoped John saw me choking his ghost. "He frustrates me.

He makes me angry. And I don't think that's a good relationship, one built on frustration and anger. Do you?"

Will shook his head somberly.

"He's good for a lay, though," I mused.

"Oh, please don't say that."

I waited for Will to explain what he meant. He just stared at me.

Then he whacked himself in the forehead with the palm of his hand. "I can't believe"—he gestured all around us—"that I'm sitting here at a spring break party on the Redneck Riviera, warning a girl not to have casual sex with my best friend. I think we've entered a parallel universe. I keep expecting people to come out of the porta-toilets with their heads on backward."

"Exactly," I said. "Stop trying. It doesn't make sense for John and me to date. It makes sense for us to do it."

"But I'm telling you, that's not how John works. He's going to want more than that from you."

"I don't have anything else to give him," I said. "Not while he's chained to the bridge."

Will took a deep breath and let out a long sigh. "I wish there were some way to unchain him from the bridge, so he could go do his art. I've been trying to figure that out for years."

"I gave it a shot."

Will eyed me, then drained his beer. "What'd you do?"

"To get out of trouble, I had to write a proposal to the DA for a project to keep other teenagers out of trouble. I suggested that they put a camera at the bridge, with a feed to the police dispatcher. That way, they'll always know when someone tries to go on the bridge. John will have no reason to check for trespassers every five minutes. And the DA said the city is actually going to do it."

Will produced another beer from beside him in his chair and took a big gulp, then glanced at me. "Sorry. I need this worse than you do, because I'm a virgin."

He was still thinking about that? "No prob." I felt bad about my virgin comment, especially when we were talking about his friend hooking up. Boys were so sensitive about odd things. And sometimes I couldn't keep my mouth shut.

"What did John say about the camera?" Will asked.

"I haven't told him. They were supposed to install it today. But I doubt it will do any good. John has a short-circuit. Logic doesn't touch that part of his brain. It's going to take more than a camera to unchain him."

I wanted to hear what Will had to say about this, because he looked worried, and he was drinking fast. But John came back then with virgin (ha ha) drinks for us, frozen coconut and pineapple juice in plastic hurricane glasses with straws and paper umbrellas and monkey figurines stuck into the ground ice. Very spring break.

We sat with the cool tide scooting past our bare feet, sipping our drinks, watching the crush of dancers inside the tiki torches. Will chatted with us about the girl trouble Rashad and Skip had gotten into during the past four days, and the escapades of some of their other high school friends—now college friends, at least to

Will. Then he made a *Star Wars* reference to John that was clearly boy-code for sex, and stood up unsteadily. "See you on Saturday at Rashad's party?" We both said yes and watched Will wander away into the crowd.

I settled closer to the John side of my chair. "You're not worried about him?"

John shook his head. "He'll go up to his room and watch movies, fall asleep. Rashad and Skip will come in with girls at about four A.M. and kick him out. He'll go run fifteen miles. That's what Will does on road trips."

"That's so sad!" Immediately I wished I could take it back. I didn't want John to think again that I was interested in Will.

I scanned his dark eyes in the moonlight. I thought I saw anger there, but no—it was lust. Oooh.

The throbbing dance beat inside the tiki torches transformed into a slow groove. John stood. "Don't be sad on spring break. Let's dance."

He led me across the sand and into the crowd of couples. This time, no mean girls gave my blue hair the evil eye. These girls were very intent on the boys they were with. More feeling up was going on than dancing.

I hoped John and I would fit right in for once. He put his arms around me, bent over with his chin resting on my shoulder, and swayed with me. As the song progressed, he slipped his hands to my waist and moved them slowly up my sides. So far so good. If his hands made it another inch, he'd be touching my boobs.

The next slow song started. Surely this would prove to be

the boob song. But wait a minute. He skipped *over* my boobs to stroke the sensitive skin on the undersides of my arms. It certainly was titillating, but it wasn't the good old-fashioned feeling-up I wanted.

I wondered why he didn't touch my boobs. Maybe he was afraid I had Stockholm Syndrome after all, the kind where your captor makes your arms tingle. Maybe he was afraid of taking advantage of me. Or maybe I had read him completely wrong all this time. He liked me as a friend and didn't *want* to touch my boobs.

"Why don't you touch my boobs?"

He took his chin off my shoulder and looked at me. "Here?" He glanced around at the other couples. "Because we're not drunk."

"Right." I tried not to sound disappointed. But the air was charged with sex, positively sparkling with it. It didn't seem fair for us to be the sober ones *and* the pristine ones.

"And it's not very original." He hooked his thumbs on either side of the waistband of my jeans, and slowly, slowly dragged his thumbs across my skin until they touched in front, just below my belly button.

Oh, God. He didn't put his hands any farther down my pants, but there was no question now of what he wanted. And he kissed me exactly as I had kissed him in the car: along my jaw, then back toward my ear.

I should have been more careful what I wished for. The claustrophobic feeling crept up on me at the same time I opened and grew hotter for John. It was the best and the worst at once, and it was going to tear me apart. I couldn't stand it much longer. God, I wished I didn't feel this way. I wished I was a different person. But I would not get trapped in our town for the rest of my life. Not even for John. We needed to get this over with.

"Are you ready to go?" I whispered.

"You're not enjoying your spring break?" he murmured before he gently bit my earlobe.

"I am, very much. But if we left now, when we got back I'd still have a couple of hours alone with you before work."

He pulled me through the crowd so fast that I got the giggles. Yes, everything would work out perfectly. We would have a one-night stand. And then, as long as I skipped Rashad's party, wore my helmet when I rode my motorcycle, and managed to stay away from the bridge until I moved to Birmingham in June, I would never see John again.

I DID GET SOME SLEEP IN the truck on the way back, despite his hand softly stroking my shoulder. I think he meant it to be soothing, but of course any part of me he touched leapt to life.

I was so beat that I slept anyway. And had wild dreams about him on the dark beach.

The truck lurched over a bump. I sat up. We'd reached Chilton County, still about twenty minutes from home. Looming over the interstate was the water tower shaped like a giant peach. Or a giant ass, depending on how sleepy you were.

I lay back down on the seat with my head on his thigh, like before. But this time, I couldn't help myself. My hand slid up the inside of his hard thigh. I didn't quite dare, because I didn't want him to tell me no. But I got very close to touching The Place Prisoners Should Not Touch Policemen.

His breath caught. I thought he was going to pick up my hand and move it back to my side of the car, where it belonged.

He didn't.

I never really went back to sleep after that. I was so alive with thoughts of what I was going to do to him, and what he was going to do to me.

At least I *thought* I didn't go back to sleep. But his door slammed, and I started up. We'd already stopped at his apartment complex. He walked around to my door and opened it, bracing his big body inside the frame. "You're too tired for this," he said gently. "Come inside and sleep."

Drat, he was trying to get out of it. At least he wasn't offering to take me home.

I shook my head. There was no way I was going to miss this. Scooting to the edge of the seat, I wrapped my legs around his hips and pulled him into a full-body embrace. I ran my fingers through his short hair, pressed his head down to mine, and kissed him.

And then he took charge.

Oh. My. God. He kissed exactly like I thought he would. Slowly. Thoroughly. Styled for her pleasure.

And I'd been dead wrong when I thought he might not like

me after all. I could tell from the way his hands grasped my hair and trembled on the back of my neck that he wanted this as much as I did.

When we pulled back to breathe, he guided me out of the car and up the stairs. Our footsteps echoed against the other apartment buildings. It was about four in the morning. Even the hum of traffic on the interstate had quieted.

He unlocked the door and held it open for me as I walked into the dark living room. Then he closed the door behind us with an official-sounding *thunk* and locked the dead bolt. And turned to me.

This was it. Almost a week of crushing on him—more like two weeks if I admitted to myself how interested I'd been in him the first night at the bridge. And today, fourteen hours of slow, grinding, up-close-and-personal pining for him. Finally, this was it.

17

He backed me up a pace and pressed me into the corner. His big middle finger stroked down my cheek, across my chin, and up to my lips. In the softest filter of streetlights through the blinds, he touched me like he really did think I was beautiful. Or at least was determined to make a good show of it. His dark eyes were so tender that I was ready to believe it.

Then he kissed me again. I opened my mouth and let him kiss me as deeply as he wanted. His hands slid down my sides and started to wander, and I let them wander where they would.

It was all good, until I flashed hot in my very small shirt, too hot. My chest pounded like I was having a heart attack. Red warning lights flashed behind my eyelids.

I pushed him away, and held on to him at the same time to keep from falling.

Dazed, he looked down at me, panting. He couldn't catch his breath. "What is it?" he whispered.

"Not in the corner," I breathed. "Anywhere but the corner."

He put his heavy arm around my shoulders and guided me across the room. I thought: Couch? Couch? Couch? No couch. We passed the living room couch and crossed the threshold into his bedroom. I thought: jackpot.

Lois's voice crackled on the humming police scanner.

I ducked from under his arm, dove across the bed, and switched the scanner off.

In the silence, I felt a wave of relief. Then it occurred to me he might be weird about keeping his scanner on at all times, listening for trouble.

I sat up cross-legged on the bed. He still watched me from the doorway, beside the large drawing of the bridge.

Since I'd already turned the scanner off and he hadn't kicked me out of his apartment yet, I considered asking him to take the bridge drawing down and deposit it in the closet, just for the next two hours. I opted not to, lest he think I was a complete fruitcake.

Wait a minute. Who was the bigger fruitcake? *He* was the one with the bridge obsession.

Okay, I did not want to hold a fruitcake bake-off just then. I wanted John to do me.

I held out my hand to him.

He approached me cautiously, beams of moonlight through the windows blinds moving over him. He thought I was going to bolt. He sat in front of me, weighing down the bed so I sank toward him a little on the mattress. With a hot palm on each of my thighs, he leaned in until our foreheads touched. Then he brushed his sensitive lips up my cheek and toward my hairline.

Here was more of what I expected from John. Tortured self-control. Now I didn't have nearly as much self-control as he did. I leaned in and kissed him hard.

We played this game for the next hour and a half. He would take over and kiss me carefully, with attention to detail, like I was one of his drawings. It was the slowest, most thorough, most agonizing, best make-out session imaginable. Until he tried to take my shirt off, or my jeans. I couldn't allow that.

Then I would take over, and things would go faster. There was also a certain amount of fascinated experimentation on my part. After his show of being a big strong policeman, it really turned me on to find out he was a normal boy after all. An unusually well-built boy, granted, but still a boy who reacted in predictable ways. When I whispered in his ear, he shivered. When I touched him, he gripped me harder. I managed to get all his clothes off while it was my turn to play authority. His beautiful naked body pressed down on me, wanting in.

I could have very happily spent a whole week in foreplay with him, but I had to leave for the diner soon. I needed to get what I'd come for.

One of the condoms I'd bought for Eric yesterday was in my pocket. If I pulled it out, I might look slut-whorish, like I was always on the ready. Anyway, I figured John was so über-responsible, he had his own. Even if he hadn't intended them for me. I rolled out from under him, opened the side table drawer, and fished inside. "How lucky," I murmured. "An assortment." I spread them out beside us on the bed to look.

"Meg, I don't think we should do it."

His soft words stabbed me. The only other sound was the sheets slipping against each other as we breathed. Suddenly I longed for the hum of cars on the interstate, even the scanner. Anything to drown out those gentle words I'd known were coming all along.

"You could have fooled me," I managed.

"I mean, I do. Of course I do. But I think there's something wrong if you want to have sex with me but you won't even take your clothes off."

I moved my hands down to zip my jeans. "I have given you access."

"You've probably still got your shoes on." I felt him exploring with his bare foot at the end of the bed. "Yes, you've still got your shoes on. So you can run out the door."

"That's not why."

"Okay, then." He propped himself up on one elbow and gazed at me. "Why won't you take your clothes off?"

I shuddered at a little chill that slipped into the warm bed with us. "I would feel naked."

"You would *be* naked."

"Exactly."

In the soft light, I watched the worry lines appear between

his eyebrows. He pulled one hand from under the covers and moved it to stroke my hair, but something in my face must have stopped him. He put his hand down. "You won't let me kiss you in the corner."

"I won't let *anybody* kiss me in the corner."

"Then you don't trust anybody. I'm not sure I want to have sex with a girl who doesn't trust me."

"You're not sure? Let me help you make the decision." I slid out of bed and landed with my shoes on the carpet, hard enough that the room shook, just to make my point.

He grabbed my wrist, his big hand tight and hot around me. "I mean, I *do* want to have sex with you, but I want you to trust me."

The red lights flashed behind my eyes again. "*Never grab me.*"

I think a few seconds passed before the red lights faded and I looked at John again. He had let me go in surprise, dark eyes wide.

"I hope I got sand in your bed," I threw at him on my way out of his bedroom.

I built speed across his living room, through the door of his apartment, and down the stairs outside. By the time my feet hit the asphalt, I was running at top speed across the parking lot and onto the shoulder of the highway. It was only about two miles to Eggstra! Eggstra! And the jog would be good for me. I hadn't gotten my run in yesterday. I probably had leukemia.

Through the trees, the interstate had begun to hum again with the traffic of early commuters to Birmingham. And footsteps rang behind me, gaining on me. John passed me and stepped in front of me. I stopped to keep from running right into him. He wore jogging shoes and jeans, no shirt. His white chest glowed under the streetlights.

He took a big breath. "You're fast."

"So they tell me." I stepped around him and started running again.

"Hey!" He ran a few steps after me and caught me with his hand around my upper arm.

I stopped and screamed at him, "I told you, don't grab me!"

"For God's sake, Meg! We look like a domestic!"

"Whose fault is that? You're the one with your shirt off."

He looked down at his bare chest, then accusingly at a passing car. Then accusingly at me. "*What* is the *problem?*"

I put my fists on my hips. Between panting breaths, I said, "All right, John. You want to play dumb? I'll explain it to you. Girls don't like it when boys don't want to have sex with them."

"I—"

"Boys are supposed to be helpless in the face of their hormones, or a pair of big tits. You didn't turn me down because I had my shoes on. That's bullshit. You're in love with someone else."

"I am *not* in love with Angie," he said with his hands out to me. "To tell you the truth, I was kind of relieved when she broke up with me. I should have ended it a long time before that, but she'd gotten to be a habit. A bad habit."

"You're in love with that dead girl."

He put his hands down. "Oh, come *on*, Meg," he shouted at me. "Why does it always circle around to that?"

"Right. Why does it?"

He ran his hands through his hair and held on to the back of his neck, both biceps bulging. God *damn* him for looking so hot when I wanted to run away.

"You reminded me of her that first night at the bridge," he said. "That's it. You didn't even remind me of her by the time I told you about her. And now you don't remind me of anyone." He squeezed his eyes shut and took a deep breath, gathering courage, before he told me. "I'm in love with *you*."

I felt the tears coming. I lashed out to keep from crying. "You love me so much that you won't do me when presented with the invite. This is all about you needing to be in control. It's not enough to arrest me. You make me ride around with you while dirty men tell me they want to rape me. It's not enough to take away my spring break. You give me back a little piece of it, but only if you hold me on a leash. It's not even enough to have sex with me."

I gasped for breath, and he stepped toward me.

"You want me to beg for it," I choked out, "so you can say no."

I wished it wasn't true. But I could tell by his silence that it was. Maybe he was just now realizing it himself.

But then he said, "That's stupid. I said no because *you* don't love *me*."

"I *do* love you," I screamed at him.

"You can't possibly! You're so closed off. You're just saying that to get laid."

He flinched and turned to look as a car swiped past us on the highway. I took the opportunity and ran.

He caught up with me in five seconds and stepped in my path. "We can't leave it like this," he said, feeling for my hand, chasing my hand around my waist when I held it away from him. "Let's talk about it when we're not mad. I'll call you later today."

I blinked back tears. "I'll still be mad later today."

"Then you call me when you're not mad anymore."

"I don't call people." I brushed past him and escaped.

This time, he let me go.

AFTER A MILE AND A HALF, I was too tired to go on. I slowed to a stop on the grassy shoulder and bent over with my hands on my knees, catching my breath. I did not have leukemia. This fatigue was of an entirely different sort.

I glanced at my watch in the moonlight. The problem with walking was, I would never make it to the trailer in time to take a shower before my shift at the diner. I needed to wash the sand and the ocean and John off me. I smelled his cologne and his sweat on my skin.

But I couldn't run anymore. I walked along the dark highway, wading through the long grass that had sprung back to life in the past few days. I should have felt scared, a teenage girl walking along the highway alone in a skimpy shirt at 5:30 A.M. I didn't.

There was no one to scare me. This section of the main highway through town was lined with pine trees and utterly abandoned. I pictured John driving up and down this highway, nineteen times a night, for the rest of his life.

I had set up my project for the DA to discourage other teenagers from venturing onto the bridge, but also to encourage John to let the bridge go and leave town. Now that I finally faced my feelings for him, I realized I'd hoped all along he would follow me to Birmingham and we'd hook back up. And now that I'd gotten up close and personal with his control freak side, I knew it wouldn't happen. My project alone wouldn't be enough to nudge him off his orbit around the bridge. He would stay. I would go, but I would feel like I'd left part of me here with him, cemented as securely as my handprint tile on the wall in the park.

This wasn't happening, this couldn't possibly be the way it ended, but it was.

Unless I did something.

With a final sigh, I started running again. I had gotten my second wind. I had a lot to do after my shift at the diner, before I finally went to bed. I needed to sweet-talk Lois. Then I would make an appointment with a train.

AND AT 6:01 THE NEXT MORNING, I called him.

"Hey!" he said. "I was just about to drive back to the police station." He sounded stoked to hear from me. Little did he know what was in store for him. "Where are you?"

"On the bridge."

Through the phone, I heard the wail of his siren begin. I also heard it in stereo, up on the highway. Somewhere beyond the bridge and the clearing and the dark silhouette of trees against the gray dawn sky, the siren woke the dead.

"John!" I shouted. "John, you don't have to do that. I looked up the schedule on the Internet. I even called to double-check. The train won't cross here for another fifteen minutes."

The siren switched off.

I joked, "And you thought I wouldn't make a good manager."

John had switched off, too. I repeated his name through the phone, but there was only static and the murmur of Lois's voice. He must have thrown the phone down on my seat.

I watched across the clearing, waiting. Finally I heard the low hum of the car's motor. Then the car itself emerged from the trees, blue lights off but headlights on. He drove too fast across the clearing and skidded to a stop in the gravel. A cloud of dust rose in front of the headlights and hung in the still dawn air.

He got out of the car, strode toward the bridge, stopped in front of the *No Trespassing* sign. I could tell from the way he moved that he hadn't seen the city's new installation before. A new sign bolted below the *No Trespassing* sign said *SMILE! You're being watched by the Police Department*. He turned around and looked for the camera mounted high on a tree.

Then he brought his phone up to his ear. "Is this your surprise for me?" His tone was absolutely flat. But he caught an extra breath at the end, like he was trying hard to stay calm.

"I figured you would have seen it by now, on one of your many trips down here to the bridge on your shift all night."

"I didn't get out of the car." He took two hard breaths in the phone. "Does the camera really feed back to the police station?"

"Yes. Lois is watching us right now. Say hi." I waved in a broad motion that the camera could pick up this far away.

"Meg, you're doing exactly what you got arrested for in the first place."

"I let Lois know what I was doing so she wouldn't tell on me. The only reason it's illegal is that it's not safe. I've already informed you that for the next fifteen minutes, it's safe."

"Somehow, I don't think the DA is going to buy that." His words sounded rational, but his voice was drawn tight underneath.

"Yeah, I should have run away from you and started college and gone on without you. But I would always have regretted it if I didn't give this a shot." I pulled back his leather cop jacket, so maybe he could see even from a distance that I was wearing his *To Protect and Serve* T-shirt. "Come and get me. You have fifteen minutes before the train comes." I glanced at my watch. "Twelve."

He was breathing so hard that he exhaled static into the phone. I could see his shoulders rising and falling in the dim light.

"Come on, John. You're the bravest person I've ever met."

In a rush, he closed the rest of the space across the clearing and put one foot on the bridge.

"Take your shoes off, so you don't get trapped," I suggested. "I want to keep you safe."

I heard him curse before he pocketed his phone and bent to unlace his boots. He cursed again, muffled, like he couldn't get them unlaced fast enough. Then he straightened and stepped in his socks across the ties, toward me.

He raised the phone to his ear. "Aren't you supposed to be at work right now?" he asked in that strange, flat voice.

"I have a few minutes. I got Purcell to stay a little late at the end of his shift."

"I thought you didn't get along that well with Purcell." He was only yards away from me, coming fast across the railroad ties, without glancing down at his feet.

"This was important."

"It took a lot of planning," he said in the strange voice. He was a few steps away. His dark eyes didn't look loving. And they didn't look afraid.

That was the first hint something was terribly wrong.

I knew I'd better start explaining myself, or I was going to be in trouble. "Now that the camera's here, there's no reason for your body to stay, guarding this bridge. But your mind would still be here. I thought it might help you to come up on the bridge, so you could stop wondering. See what the dead girl saw."

This was likely not what she saw. I didn't know what time of day those kids got creamed, but if they were drunk, it was probably night. The nighttime view from the bridge was beautiful, but there wasn't a whole lot to see, surrounded by darkness. So I'd banked on bringing John here at sunrise, when we could see more.

And I was right. The faintest hint of pink in the sky reflected far below us in the river, flat as glass. Mist rose from the water and curled up to me. Dark pines and trees with new green leaves clung desperately to the violent angle of the gorge.

I put my phone down. "And feel what they felt." As John stepped close to me, I put my other hand on his bare arm.

"Don't touch me," he barked.

I looked into his hard eyes. My heart skipped a beat as I recognized that look. The look Eric had gotten in his eyes when I pushed him beyond control, and nothing but anger was left.

"John," I said quickly. "I'm sorry. I thought—"

"Poor judgment." He snapped a cold handcuff around my wrist.

I fought him without thinking, with the vaguest awareness that I'd struck him and hurt him somehow. Then my shoulder hit the rusty wall of the trestle, and the *bang* echoed against the hills. Through blinking red lights, I was looking over at the pink river, watching both our cell phones fall into the mist.

Already I was half gone, wondering whether the fish would run up my minutes, when he said, "Don't resist arrest," and slapped the handcuff around my other wrist.

18

I was a skeleton. I leaned over Meg's hospital bed, the Meg that used to be. She slept. I reached down and brushed pink hair away from her face. It came out in a clump, and the strands slipped through my finger bones.

"After?" said Lois.

"John!" said Lois.

The second time, I roused enough to know Lois was calling on John's radio attached to his shirt. John had slung me over his hard shoulder, which dug into my belly with each step he took. Nose to his back, I smelled his sweat. Strange that I recognized his scent so readily. But there was no cologne mixed with it. He'd become someone else.

"I can see you on camera, John," said Lois. "I saw what you did."

SLOWLY I REALIZED I WAS IN the backseat of the police car, on my stomach, face stuck to the vinyl. Men murmured outside.

The talking escalated as the door opened behind me. "That's why she passed out." I recognized the voice of Quincy, my paramedic friend. "Uncuff her, would you?"

I felt the cuffs slide off my wrists, but I still couldn't move.

"Why does she do that?" Officer Leroy asked.

"Panic attack." I felt Quincy leaning over me. "Come here, you rascal."

My face peeled away from the vinyl. He slid me backward across the seat and picked me up. I clung to him with his shirt bunched in both my fists, like he was my father.

"You need to get over this, sugar," he murmured. "It's completely psychosomatic. You were sick four years ago." He set me on the back bumper of the ambulance and held me steady with one hand while he reached for something.

"Not the—" The smelling salts razored through my nostrils and into my brain. At least I could see clearly again: Quincy standing in front of me, weathered face lined with concern, and Officer Leroy hovering behind him.

"Where's John?" I asked.

"Where's John," Officer Leroy muttered. He shook his finger at me. "John is having his own panic attack. That's a nice stunt you pulled, missy. You know his brother got killed on that bridge."

I tried to gasp, but it was so hard to breathe. "His *brother?*" I coughed out.

Quincy caught me as I started forward. Over his shoulder, he said to Officer Leroy, "You could maybe wait to tell her that later."

"John said it was a girl who lived in his neighborhood," I wailed.

"Right," said Officer Leroy. "That was his brother's girlfriend."

"Oh God." I tried to stand up, but Quincy pressed me back, saying, "Easy, now."

"And that's just between us," Officer Leroy insisted. "Most folks on the force don't know, or they don't understand that's why After joined. If the chief found out, he might kick After off. This is After's whole life, and you persist in treating it like it's a *joke?*" Officer Leroy stepped closer to me like he wanted to throttle me. When Quincy put his hands up, motioning for Officer Leroy to back off, Officer Leroy raised his voice and shouted at me instead. "Don't you go over there. You don't poke at a snake. You try to go over to him again and I'll handcuff you myself."

It all made sense now. A father who had moved to Colorado. A mother who had moved to Virginia because she couldn't stand it anymore. A framed family portrait from ten years back, with a brother who had also left town—except John had not made clear exactly where his brother had gone. A black handprint on the colorful wall in the park when John was nine.

I'd gotten so used to hearing it in the past week that I didn't even notice the low hum until the train sounded its deafening horn. We all turned to look. John stood with his back to us at the rail in front of the bridge. His head was bowed. He didn't look up at the train. He didn't cover his ears.

The low hum I thought I'd been hearing for the past two weeks had been the train in John's head all along.

I crossed my arms and hugged myself, but it was no use. I whispered, "What have we done to each other?"

I DID SOMETHING I HADN'T DONE since sophomore year, when the doctor told me I was in remission. I cried.

I cried so much that Quincy didn't want to let me ride to Eggstra! Eggstra! on my motorcycle. There was no way I was getting in the ambulance at that point, much less a cop car. He finally settled for letting me ride my motorcycle and following me in the ambulance, with Officer Leroy behind him. We left John at the bridge.

I cried as I tripped through the door of the trailer and tore off John's police jacket and *To Protect and Serve* T-shirt, which had begun to sear my skin. Of course, I had to wear something to work, but laundry had not been high on my priority list for the past week.

The first shirt I grabbed from my closet was my Cookie

Monster T-shirt. I'd always loved the CM, an uninhibited glutton who lived like he was dying. I'd stopped wearing the T-shirt when I dyed my hair blue because the CM and I matched a little too well. But I didn't have time to search for something else this morning. Purcell had already stayed almost an hour late for me.

I cried as I burst through the door of Eggstra! Eggstra!, shoulders squared for the huge argument I was about to have with Purcell that would send half the customers running from the packed diner. But when Purcell and Corey saw me, they both left food burning to rush over to me and ask what was wrong.

I cried harder. Their anger I could have dealt with. I didn't know what to do with sympathy. "I'm okay. I'm fine," I choked out. "Just a little teen angst. Nothing to see here."

Corey ran back to the grill to flip the ham, then reluctantly raked it into the trash. Purcell still stood next to me. Looking at the floor, he mumbled, "Take another hour. I can stay."

"Oh, no. Working will help me. And you've stayed so long already." I wiped at the tears under my eyes. "Do you want me to teach you to read?"

He looked as shocked as I felt at hearing myself. I went on, "I don't know how to teach someone to read, but there are workbooks and stuff I can check out of the high school library. Are you on day shift next week?"

He nodded.

"We can do it after school, in the lull before the dinner crowd."

He held up his fist. I wasn't sure what to do, but I touched his fist with my fist. This seemed to be right, because he took off his apron and headed out the door. I guessed he had accepted my offer with thanks. It was hard to tell, since we'd just now become friends.

I tried to dry up as Corey and I cooked breakfast for the throngs of people from the car factory who got off work at 7 A.M. and the travelers headed home from spring break. But every time I saw the reflection of my Cookie Monster T-shirt in the toaster, I wanted to pull my hair out.

Hours later, toward the end of my shift, after the lunch crowd had thinned, I called Tiffany. Again, I didn't know who was more shocked: Tiffany, that I was calling her, or me, that I was calling her. Soon she be-bopped in and slid onto a stool at the counter.

I poured her a cup of coffee. "Sorry to drag you up here on your one weekend of spring break left."

"No prob. It's not like I have a boyfriend to hang out with or something. I've been asleep since Thursday." She eyed the coffee. I moved the cream and sugar toward her as a hint. She mixed some in clumsily, like a coffee virgin. Then she looked up at me, and her face fell into concern. "Oh my God, Meg, what's wrong?"

What *wasn't* wrong? I told her the whole story of how John took me to the beach, we almost had sex, I induced his nervous breakdown accidentally, and he gave me a panic attack on purpose.

When I finished, she sat blinking at me for a few seconds. Then she exclaimed, "*You had sex with Johnafter?*"

I glanced around the diner at the patrons trying not to stare at us. "I told you, no," I said quietly. "But I saw the promised land."

She looked right into my eyes with a steady gaze. "Is he a good kisser?"

I held her gaze. "John does *everything* well." Then I watched my hand wipe absently at the counter. "I should set the record straight about something I said to you on the phone Wednesday. I still don't think it's a good idea for you to have sex with Brian just to get back together with him. But since you came to me for sex advice, I want to revise what I told you about sex not being any good. With Eric, I was half thinking about something else. With John, there was nothing but John. The frontal lobes fizzled out on me, and only the trusty old medulla was still operating. There was nothing going on but breathing"—I took in a deep breath and let it out slowly—"and touching. Now I can see how sex could be really, really fantastic if the guy was slow and caring and thorough and obviously very into you, and if you were in love." I was so tired of crying by then that I watched with a weird detachment as my tears plopped onto the countertop in small wet circles.

"How are you going to get him back?" Tiffany asked.

I sniffled. "That's why I called you. I want to dye my hair its natural color. Of course, *natural color* is a relative term. When I get off work in a minute, will you go across the street to the drugstore with me and help me figure out what shade my hair used to be?"

"Wow," Tiffany said. "It's hard to remember back that far.

Wasn't it dark brown? And with your blue eyes, you're going to look striking. Wow." She took a sip of her coffee and grimaced. "You think dying your hair will get Johnafter back?"

I glanced at my reflection in the toaster. "I think it will help me connect with him. You know, John's going to live in this town forever. And there's nothing I'd less rather do. But I'm almost to the point with him that I'd be willing to live in a triple-wide and bake warm fruit cobbler for him and listen to the police scanner while he was at work."

Tiffany choked on her coffee. "You *are?*"

"No, I'm definitely not. I *almost* am. I'll never quite get there. I have too much fear of becoming my parents. But I feel this connection with John. I can't discount him just because it's inconvenient. And it *would* be inconvenient. I want to go to college. I want to live in Key West. I want to see the world. But I think if I keep going at this rate, I'll see the world by myself. I'll move to Key West by myself, and live there by myself, and leave again by myself. I never realized that's what I've been doing. I mean, look at my hair. I get along here in town because people here have always known me. No one at college will know me. And if you see someone you don't know with blue hair, around here where the manga aesthetic is hardly the norm, what do you think to yourself? Blue hair says *stay away from me.*" I ran my fingers down one strand and held it out in front of my eyes to study it. "But you think if I dye it brown right after all this happened with John, it will look like I'm desperate to get him back?"

"No," she said slowly. "Not now that you've explained it. I think it will look like you've finally decided you're not dying of leukemia."

Oh.

My parents would be happy about that.

As they were driving away to Graceland, I had asked my dad to bring me back a fried peanut butter and banana sandwich. He told me they weren't bringing me shit. My mom would probably try to sneak me a teddy bear wearing an Elvis T-shirt or something equally cutesy anyway. But when they got back tomorrow night and saw my brown hair, yeah. They would wish they'd bought me that blue jean jacket with the Graceland mansion Bedazzled on the back, I just knew it. And then I would sit them down and have a heart-to-heart with them, and I would apologize. For everything.

Tiffany pushed her coffee away. "When do you think you'll see John again? Are you planning to rob a bank?"

"Ha. He may be at a college party in Birmingham tonight. That was the other reason I called you. I need you to go with me."

"No way," she said. "I don't want to drink."

"Believe me, I don't want you to drink. Ever. Again. You don't have to drink. A college party isn't that big a deal. It's a lot like a high school party. The boys are still stupid. They're just taller and hold their liquor better."

"Why do I have to go with you?" she whined.

"I'm not positive John will be there. He might stay away to

avoid seeing me. And Eric might be there. You know how drunk he'll be. It would help if I went with someone to run interference for me."

"Meg, if you think John won't be there and Eric will, robbing a bank sounds like a better idea to get John's attention."

I shook my head. Blue strands fell into my eyes. I pushed them out of my face in annoyance. "Will Billingsley will be there. I need to talk to him. We've had a few chats about John and the bridge, and he never warned me about John's brother."

"Will Billingsley?" She perked up and leaned forward. "I used to have a little crush on Will Billingsley. We were on the debate team together."

I rolled my eyes. "I swear, Tiff, if my ass made good grades, you'd want to date my ass."

"Hey!" She slapped her hand on the counter. "You have a thing for jail. You date boys in it, and you date boys who put other boys in it. I have a thing for good grades. Which is more healthy?"

"That settles it," I said. "Tonight we'll go on a boy-hunt together. Maybe this outing will turn out better than our last outing."

"My first college party." She put her chin in her hand and studied me. "Are you getting an apartment near the university in the summer? Do you have a roommate yet? I don't have a roommate."

I rubbed at a knot of tension in the back of my neck. "You mean, we would sign a lease together?"

"Think of all the fun we'll have!" Tiffany gushed. "We'll shop.

We'll go dancing. We'll giggle about our strange taste in boys. You'll get me in trouble. I'll keep you out of trouble. It will be perfect!"

"I'm not good at plans," I said. "I gave it a shot this morning. I made a plan to cure John of the bridge, and you see how *that* worked out."

"But it was your first time. The first time isn't so good."

I snorted. "A day of firsts for you. You just made your first sex joke. Congratulations." I held out my hand.

She shook my hand across the counter. "Roomie."

Part of me wanted to jerk my hand away in revulsion, but this was not polite. And more of me looked forward to having a . . . friend. "Roomie, maybe. Yes, okay, roomie."

"Hooray!" She let go of my hand and put both her arms up to signal a touchdown. "Now if you and John could make up at the party tonight, it wouldn't be such a bad spring break after all."

"I doubt he'll be there," I admitted. "But just in case he is, I don't want to stand him up."

19

To get a space, Tiffany had to park all the way down at the Devil fountain at Five Points. She and I hiked past the ornate 1920s façades in our grown-up heels and clubbing dresses. The trees along the sidewalk budded spring flowers in the cool night.

With every step, I felt another tingle of anticipation. I hoped John would be at the party. I hoped against hope he would like my new look. And then, when we turned the corner and I saw his truck—well, you would have thought I was horny for Fords. I wanted to *run* up the steps and into Rashad's apartment. Which would have been decidedly uncool.

Buzz-kill of the evening: just up the hill from John's truck was Eric's Beamer.

Rashad greeted us at the door and welcomed us into his

home. He met Tiffany cordially. He raised his eyebrows at my hair and told me he'd always had a soft spot for brunettes. But behind him, the party degenerated into college. Life-size posters of Jimi Hendrix covered the walls. Beaded curtains hung in the doorways. Christmas lights outlined the windows. The stereo blasted Kanye West. Couples made out in the corners, and knots of people laughed together and sipped beer.

As I wove through the crowd, leading Tiffany, searching for John, I recognized a few people who used to go to my high school. If they'd worn their jeans too short before, they'd figured out the proper length when they came to college. If they'd teased their hair up to Jesus before, city living had taught them about straightening serum. At a party back in our town, they would have talked about deer hunting, or the half-price sale on eyeliner at Target. Now, between beats of the music, I caught snippets of conversation about Harper Lee, and Condoleezza Rice, who had grown up in Birmingham, and Alabama's ex-governor who was in and out of jail (it happened to the best of us). Philosophical college conversation.

It was so cool!

I hoped John didn't miss it.

Tiffany and I emerged into the kitchen. I braced myself for John to appear when the refrigerator door closed. But it was only Will, holding a pitcher.

"Tiffany Hart!" he hollered.

"Will Billingsley!" She tilted her head in that way I'd found so annoying when she did it to John. Now it was cute.

Will gestured with the pitcher. "I was pouring myself some iced tea. Would you like some tea?"

She wrinkled her nose. "Is there booze in it?"

He looked into the pitcher. "Just tea. No imbibing for me tonight. I have two papers due Monday. Homework over spring break. Can you believe that?"

"No!" she exclaimed, stepping closer to him. *I do my homework* clearly was the mating call for their species. "Yes, I would love some tea."

He turned to me. "And—I'm sorry—how about your frien—" As our eyes met, he started back. "Meg! I didn't recognize you." He frowned and held the pitcher away from me. "No tea for you. How could you do that to John? I got home from the beach at four this morning, and he shows up at my apartment at eight, distraught, fully armed, waving his nightstick!"

Tiffany put both hands over her mouth. She moved them away to say, "Oh my God," then put them back.

"I didn't know his brother got killed," I hissed, lowering my voice in case John was sneaking around. "Why the hell didn't you tell me?"

"You *did* know his brother got killed!" Will insisted. "You and I had a conversation about this at the beach. You compared John to Mulder searching for his lost sister. I know I remember. I wasn't *that* drunk."

"I was talking about *The X-Files*! It was an analogy, a very loose analogy!"

"Oh," he said, and his shoulders relaxed. "Well, this morning,

I convinced him otherwise. I also made him believe you're a manipulative bitch. Sorry."

I was gearing up to tell Will what I thought of him when I was attacked from behind. Eric picked me up, put me on the countertop, and pushed his hips between my legs. Which was all the more offensive because the skirt of my dress was short. Leering at me with red-rimmed eyes, he leaned in and whispered in my ear, "Is your ride-along with John over?"

He was going to ask me if I needed a new ride. If he asked me if I needed a new ride, I was going to slap him.

"Do you need a new—"

I raised my hand.

He caught both my wrists in his hands and squeezed. Hard.

I leaned around him. "Tiffany," I called, trying not to sound desperate. "Remember why I brought you here?"

"Unhand her, dumbass," Will yelled across the kitchen.

With a sidelong glance at Will, Eric let go of my wrists and backed up a pace.

"My ride-along with John is not necessarily over," I told him haughtily.

Eric made a face. "You mean you're fucking the fuzz?"

"Not yet. But check back with me." Since he was still practically between my thighs, I decided this might be a good time to ask a question that had been bothering me for the past few hours. If I was nice enough at first, and he was stoned enough, maybe I'd get a straight answer. "Did you know John's brother was the boy who died on the bridge?"

Eric shrugged. "Sure. Everybody knows that. It happened when we were in third, maybe fourth grade."

"And when you suggested that we go to the bridge, was that because you knew John would find us down there and freak out?"

"Not the first time," he said. "I didn't know then that he watches the place. But when you and I parked down there, yeah." He met my gaze, with absolutely no shame.

I went cold in the tiny kitchen, and the beat of music from the next room seemed to swell louder. I couldn't believe I'd ever thought Eric and I were a lot alike. "That's evil," I said.

"You ain't seen evil yet."

I thought he was going to grab my crotch or something, and I jumped down from the counter to prevent such an unfortunate event. But he didn't try. He just walked out of the kitchen.

"Meg, when do you want to get our apartment?" Tiffany called. "I know you always say you're leaving town as soon as you can in June, on graduation night. But Will thinks it would be easier for us to get a lease starting on July first." They were standing very close together. The pitcher of tea sat on the countertop, forgotten.

I walked over to them, nodding. "That would be okay. I can stand to hang around town a few extra weeks. I may try to enjoy my last few months of high school. I might even go to the prom, if I had a date."

Tiffany's eyes sparkled at Will, like she knew who *her* prom date was, if she could argue a college boy into coming.

Will leaned back against the cabinets, grinning at her. "What's your major going to be?"

"Either English or pre-med."

"English or pre-med," he mused. "That's quite a spread. Let me give you a hint. Next fall, don't go around telling people you're majoring in English or pre-med. You'll sound like a freshman."

"Oh, yeah?" I asked. "What are *you* majoring in?"

"Chemistry," he said defensively. "Or interpretive dance." He winked at Tiffany.

She beamed. "I was going to major in English," she explained. "But I've had a life-changing experience that makes me think I might want to go into medicine. I've been riding around in an ambulance all week."

Will leaned forward and asked conspiratorially, "Were you one of the naughty ones on the bridge?"

Tiffany smiled a secret smile.

"You don't *look* naughty," Will said. He gestured to me. "This one, I can understand, but *you?* What's your GPA?"

"It's 4.0," she said.

"You're the freaking valedictorian?" he exclaimed.

She just grinned. "What's *your* GPA?"

"It's a 3.75 right now, and I'm trying to bring it up to a 3.85 this semester." He shook his head sadly. "The freshman flunk classes really did a number on me. I only made a *B* last semester in calculus—"

I interrupted, "Let me just stop the two of you right here and tell you that you disgust me. You're both so freaking well-adjusted. Why don't you skip over this part and get a joint retirement fund?"

They both turned to me with wide eyes. Then Tiffany told me she might not want to room with me after all, at the same time Will grumbled, "She's just upset about Johnafter." He put his arm around me and hugged my shoulders. "I wish I could tell you that it would work out between you two. But you did this yourself, before I was involved this morning. I'm afraid you got on the wrong side of his temper."

"What temper?" I asked before I thought. The John I'd ridden with for a week was very even-keeled, with a high threshold for suspects cussing at him, or blue-haired delinquents pushing his buttons. Then I remembered how he'd looked as he yelled at Brian and Eric at the bridge. I remembered how his knuckles had turned white on the grate in the cop car as he told me, *If I had pulled Eric out of the car myself, I'm afraid of what I would have done to him.*

"Don't do it, John," Angie's shrill voice called from the next room. "Eric's just messing with you."

John was in the kitchen doorway. Funny, I half expected to see him in his cop uniform, but he was wearing faded jeans and a green T-shirt that hugged his chest. Maybe it was the reflection from the shirt, or his eyes really were more hazel than brown, and I hadn't noticed when he wore his dark blue uniform. But now his eyes looked green.

Angie clung to him from behind, making a helpless show of holding him back.

He saw me and did a double take. But he didn't bask in my newfound beauty nearly as long as he should have. Almost immediately, his gaze flicked to Will and hardened into the dangerous, dead-eyed look. I saw myself through his eyes: dark hair, low-cut dress, with Will's arm around me.

"Oh, *that* temper," I said.

Will looked up at John, stepped away from Tiffany and me, and backed up a pace. "Rashad!" he called. He looked behind him, but he was against the wall. There was nowhere left to go.

John was across the room, on top of Will. Tiffany and I both put our hands between them before we were able to think through that unwise move. At least it temporarily kept John from hitting Will. John only gripped Will's shirt, pulled him upward, then whacked him down against the floor.

"Get *off* me, After," Will roared, red-faced. "You have completely lost it. Rashad!"

There was not enough room in the tiny kitchen for all these enormous boys, but somehow Rashad squeezed in and said, "Easy, big guy," as he pulled one of John's arms. Skip gripped John's other elbow and said in the Schwarzenegger voice, "You're terminated."

John seemed to be easing up, letting them drag him backward. Then he shook them off and went for Will again. They dove after him in a sprawl of boy on the kitchen floor.

Finally Tiffany stamped her foot and squealed, "John, he wasn't even hitting on Meg. He was hitting on me! Right, Will?"

"Right!" Will's agonized voice came from the bottom of the pile.

"But Eric said—" John's muffled voice trailed off. He erupted from the pile. With the briefest glance at me, he stalked out of the kitchen, brushing against Eric behind Angie in the doorway.

"Still looking for a fight?" Eric called after him. "You're pretty chicken without the entire police force behind you."

"Shut up, Eric," John's voice echoed. The door slammed louder than the beat of Kanye West.

I pushed past everyone, not even noticing who I was pushing past, but I heard Will breathing hard right behind me. "What are we going to do?" Tiffany panted as we dashed through the door of Rashad's apartment and down the stairs outside, into the cool night. "Are we going to chase him in my car?"

"We'll never catch him if he doesn't want to be caught." Will stopped dead at the bottom of the stairs. "His truck's still here."

"Where would he have gone?" I cried, looking up and down the empty street.

"He likes the fountain down at Five Points," Will said. We all ran down to the corner and stopped again.

The fountain was straight ahead. Behind a low circular wall, rabbits and frogs listened to the ram reading evil stories to them. I couldn't see John's face across the intersection, but I recognized his green T-shirt. He was up in the center of the fountain, sitting on the lap of the Devil.

"He *really* likes the fountain," Will said.

Even Tiffany asked, "What the hell?"

"Great," I said. "I'm finally acting sane, and John goes crazy." I turned to Will. "He's not one of those big-headed cops who carries cuffs hidden on him when he's off duty, is he? I didn't feel any cuffs on him Thursday night."

"No," Will said. "But I'll go with you if you're scared of him."

I turned back to study John, sitting motionless in the fountain. "No thanks." Crossing the street, I called over my shoulder, "I'm no more scared of him than he is of me."

John watched me coming. I stopped at the wall around the fountain. He glowered down at me from the ram's lap, arms folded. The legs of his jeans were wet from the frog statues spitting at him. An unlit cigarette hung from his lips.

I cupped my hands around my mouth like a megaphone. "Move off the Devil, toward my voice."

His expression didn't change. The cigarette quivered in the corner of his mouth as he said, "I'm trying to think like you."

I laughed. "If you were trying to think like me, you'd be turned around, straddling the Devil."

"Or Will," he said. "Or Eric."

My stomach knotted again at the thought of me and Eric. Surely John didn't believe by now that I had the hots for Eric, or Will, either. But he obviously believed Eric and I were alike. Just as I'd told him in the first place.

I said, "I had no idea about your brother."

He winced. I hated to hurt him. Again. But at least his glower was gone.

He took the cigarette out of his mouth and leaned forward with his fists on his knees. "Even if you didn't, Meg, how could you *do* that to me?"

It was my turn to wince. I stepped back from the wall of the fountain with the force of the blow. I said lamely, "I can't stay in that town, John. But I love you, and I can't leave you there." I stepped forward to the wall again. "I swear I didn't know about your brother, though. If I'd known, I would have come up with something else. Dynamited the bridge."

"Mmph," he said. "I know you didn't. Will told me you did—"

"He was wrong," I said quickly. "He is very sorry, and also his ass is grass."

"—but then I had dinner with Leroy," John went on, "and he told me you didn't know. So I went to Rashad's hoping to see you, and I've spent the past few hours making all these great plans for you and me. And then Eric told me you were with Will." He shook his head. "He tried for years. Eric finally got me."

I walked to the side of the fountain nearest the rabbit, where I was as close as I could get to John without crossing the moat between us. "What kind of plans?"

He squeezed his eyes shut, then shook his head and opened those dark eyes again, watching me. They weren't green anymore. They were back to the familiar, beautiful brown. "I'm glad it happened. I mean, I wish it hadn't happened in exactly that way. But something had to happen to make me see. I thought I was protecting people. When I handcuffed you, I realized I've let the bridge turn me into a monster. It might be good for me to get out of that town."

I gaped at him for a few seconds, honestly not believing at first that I'd heard him say this. Then I laughed. Really laughed. "No!" I said sarcastically.

He grinned. "I plan to ask Will if I can move in with him this summer. And I'm joining the university track team. I was thinking you might want to, too."

I gasped in horror. "*Join? A team?*"

"You're running five miles a day anyway," he said. "You might as well join the track team and get more scholarship money."

"That actually sounds like"—I swallowed—"fun."

"I know we need money for rent and stuff. But if we can save enough, this summer or next summer, maybe you and I could go to Europe. I could show you what I've done, and we could discover some new places together."

"I do hope you mean that in the dirtiest sense possible." I'd had enough crying for one day, so I shut my eyes and willed the tears away.

Had I fallen into the parallel universe Will had talked about at the beach? I looked around me at the majestic church behind the fountain, the bohemian storefronts, Tiffany and Will talking under a flowering tree. The dark blue sky above me seemed infinite.

John sat up, took a deep breath, and sighed. "So you like my plans?"

"I like your plans," I said. "I like having plans with you. Now come down off the Devil. It's illegal."

He jumped from ram to rabbit, paused to balance the cigarette in a turtle's mouth, stepped on a spitting frog, made it to the wall in front of me, and jumped down beside me.

And then I heard a low hum. I glanced around desperately. When the blue lights and siren burst on, the cop car was already bearing down on us in the intersection.

"Let me do the talking," I yelled to John over the wail. "I have a way with cops."

"Yes, you do," he growled at me as the cop car blew past us and kept going up the hill. "They weren't after me. You don't use your siren for college students in the fountain. Thanks for taking up for me, though." He wrapped one arm around my waist, pulled me close, and ran his fingers down a lock of my hair. "You're the bravest person I've ever met." His dark eyes gave me the loving look. The look I'd longed for.

I shivered at the chill that traveled from my scalp through my body and all the way down to my toes. "You haven't told me what you think of my hair."

He chose another lock and twisted it around his finger. "I liked it better cyan."

"Really? Then that was a complete waste of six dollars and ninety-nine cents."

"No, not really," he laughed. "Are you kidding? Now everyone can see what I saw all along."

He wrapped his big arms more tightly around me and leaned down. I caught the scent of his cologne. His warm, sensitive lips met mine.

And the rest is happily ever After.

THE NEXT NIGHT, JOHN CAME TO the diner around ten. Watching him park the cop car, I tried to look cool and aloof behind the counter. But considering what we'd done with each other after Rashad's party, there was no way. I grinned like an idiot as he hung his leather cop jacket on the coatrack. When he turned around, he grinned back at me, showing his dimples.

This cop was my boyfriend. Weird!

He squeezed between two bar stools and came right up to the counter. I stood on my tiptoes and leaned forward to kiss him. His lips touched mine, pressed harder. The tip of his tongue grazed my lips, so slowly. I shuddered. Even though Bonita was in the back clocking out and I had only two customers sitting over at the Princess Diana table, we couldn't very well get into it here in the diner, with John in uniform. But I'd never wanted someone so badly, and I could tell he felt the same.

He broke the kiss, set his forehead against mine for a moment, and finally pulled back. "Didn't you work all morning? I was afraid you wouldn't be here."

"I thought you might come in at the beginning of your shift. I didn't want to miss you."

His lips pursed ever so slightly. He reached across the counter to stroke my hair away from my face.

I actually giggled. God! "You've got me so whipped, I can't think of a single sarcastic thing to say."

"That makes me feel powerful and manly. Don't worry. I'm sure you'll think of something." He glanced at the chalkboard on the back wall. "What's the Meg Special?"

"Cobbler." I nodded to a bar stool. "Have a sit-down so we can talk while I cook."

Already taking a step toward the Elvis table, he jerked his thumb over his shoulder. "Sorry. Can't have my back to the window."

"I dare you."

He raised his eyebrows at me. "You *dare* me, huh?" Biting his lip, he slid onto the stool.

"*I* can see out the window," I assured him. "I'll watch for perps." To make good on my promise, I leaned to one side to look past his shoulder at the parking lot. A car pulled into the space beside his cop car.

He watched me closely. "I can't stand it. What is it, perps?" He turned around to look.

"My parents." They'd parked here rather than at the trailer because the suspense was killing them. They needed to make sure I hadn't burned down the diner while they were gone. Thanks for the vote of confidence. I gave my dad a thumbs-up.

He stared at me. My mom turned to him in the car, asking him, *What? What is it?* He kept staring at me. My brown hair was an even bigger shock for him than I'd expected.

I smiled and waved at him and mouthed, "Welcome home."

He put his hand to his eyes. He knew I was finally cured.